The Teens Book of Love Stories

'She first saw the boy in Red Square. There was no snow yet, but it was bitterly cold. He was certainly good-looking, thought Jane, in a stocky interesting Russian way. Then, quite suddenly, without her noticing, it happened . . . "Meet me" he whispered. And to her amazement, he told her where.'

A wonderful collection of true life love-stories from some very distinguished writers of teenage fiction.

The Teens Book
of Love Stories

Foreword by
K. M. PEYTON

Edited by Miriam Hodgson

A Magnet Book

For JRH and ECH

First published in 1987
by Methuen Children's Books Ltd
under the title *Summer of Ladybirds and other love stories*
This Methuen Teens paperback edition first published 1988
by Methuen Children's Books Ltd
A Division of OPG Services Limited
Michelin House, 81 Fulham Road, London SW3 6RB
This volume © 1987 Methuen Children's Books
Printed in Great Britain by
Cox & Wyman Ltd, Reading

ISBN 0 416 11962 X

Extract from *A Room with a View* by E. M. Forster
by kind permission of Edward Arnold (Publishers) Ltd

Contents

'She has learned what it is
to love: the greatest lesson, some
people will tell you, that our earthly
life provides.'
A Room With a View
E.M. Forster

Foreword

When one is first afflicted by the pangs of love at the age of, perhaps, fifteen – or thirteen, or eighteen – the symptoms are not treated with much sympathy by the older generation. 'Calf-love' they call it, and laugh. One's mother can be very patronizing: 'You'll get over it! It's not the real thing – it's only calf-love.' The attitude enflames: what does she know about it? Either she never knew, or she's forgotten. Early love can be shattering at the time. I can remember weeping torrents. 'You can't go out with him, you've got your homework to do. You're too young.' The agony of the boy who isn't interested, preferring one's friend . . . there was one called Colin, who loved my friend and she couldn't stand him. Just my luck – the one who loved me was a phlegmatic young man who worked on a farm and took my hand in his calloused palm when we were muck-spreading. I thought it funny and laughed, and he was mortified. Such cruelty, such pain . . . but the adults see no drama and are irritated by the tantrums, the ecstasies and the despair.

I ran away from home to get married. In those days one had to have one's parents' permission up to the age of twenty-one. I ran away a week after my twenty-first birthday, stealing my birth certificate out of my parents' desk. I changed trains twice to throw off possible pursuit and met my husband-to-be, as arranged, on Woking station. The following morning we met to proceed to the registry office, but he appeared in a navy-blue suit, which stunned me. I had never seen him in a suit before. I said I couldn't marry him in that suit so he went and changed back into his ordinary clothes.

It seems funny now but it was very serious at the time. It was a real live love story – they are going on all the time. I used to write love stories when I was still at school, and the best one I wrote was about a young woman during the war on her way to Buckingham Palace with her husband who was to receive the Victoria Cross (no half-measures in my stories). The story accompanied them on the journey, and only by what I considered a masterly twist at the end did one discover that the woman was alone, the husband only in her memory, for the award was to be made post-humously. It was a colossal tear-jerker.

I was very proud of this story and passed it to my friend to read in a French lesson. She read it and passed it on to another interested party, but unfortunately the French teacher, a very fierce lady called Miss Buist, noticed the engrossed reading going on and asked for the document to be delivered to her desk. At the end of the lesson I asked if I could have it back but my request was refused. 'I am confiscating it,' she said. It was my only copy and I was heartbroken. Did she read it? Did it get passed round the staff room to be laughed at, or merely stuffed under a pile of French translation? I never knew. But on the last day of term she gave it back to me with what, as an author, I would have described as an enigmatic smile.

Such sentimental fantasy is not the style today – nor, quite possibly, then. In this age of freedom and scepticism it is much harder to write a love story. Yet, beneath the facade of the moment, human nature remains for ever the same; the quivering uncertainties of early love have not changed. Writers have the same material to use, whatever current style it is fashionable to work in.

So, enjoy these stories, as I have. They all emphasize how much it matters, as it always did, and always will.

K. M. PEYTON

Second-best Boy

It's a shock to find that you dislike your best friend. Positively hate her. There she sat on the other side of the café table, sipping a strawberry milkshake, and shining. Trust her to hog the only patch of sunlight that managed to struggle through the dirty window.

They had met over five years ago, when they were both new and a little lost in the hurly-burly of the Comprehensive.

'Do you know anyone here?' Cathy had asked.

'No,' Rebecca said.

'Nor do I. I'm Cathy Sharwood. Let's be friends.'

And they had been friends, true friends, equals, Rebecca thought sadly, until . . . when had it happened? When had Cathy changed from a fat, cheerful carrot-top into this flower-garden of a girl, with her bright marigold hair, eyes like dark, wet pansies and a mouth like a blooming rose? This honeyed boy-trap, this pretty hypocrite.

She even smelled of flowers now, though that came out of a bottle labelled 'Geranium Girl'. A cheap scent, Rebecca thought, sniffing. And she longed for the old Cathy, who had smelled of soap and peppermint, and whose feet, newly released from hot running-shoes, stank like everybody else's.

'But you must come, you must,' Cathy was saying
now, opening her eyes very wide – as if they were not
large enough already. The milkshake had left a soft froth,
like pink cuckoo spit, on her rosy mouth. 'I said you
would. Jonathan's got his dad's car, and he's bringing a
friend . . .'

A friend? Forgotten his name, have you? That figures,
Rebecca thought bitterly. She'd made up foursomes with
Cathy before and she knew that the extra boy would be
eminently forgettable. Whether fat and greasy or thin and
earnest, he would certainly be both dull and resentful, as
unwilling to accept second-best as she was herself.

In the mirror behind Cathy's head, Rebecca saw her
own face reflected dimly, like a faded watercolour.
Nothing wrong with it. On a good day, she sometimes
thought it looked quite pretty. But beside Cathy's
glowing face, it appeared washed out, as if her own subtle
colours had been drained away to add to the gaudy
splendour of her friend.

'Becky, what's the matter?' Cathy asked, her soft eyes
looking almost convincingly innocent and bewildered. 'I
thought you'd be pleased. Don't you like Jonathan Drake?'

Bitch, Rebecca thought. Don't pretend you don't
know. Don't tell me you've never noticed how I blush
whenever I see him. Don't tell me you've never noticed
how I gulp and stammer if he asks me the time or what's
on at the local cinema. Once he rested his hand on my
shoulder and I trembled so much that you asked me, in
front of him, if I was sickening for something. I could
have killed you.

I never washed that blouse. The imprint of his hand is
still on it, folded away in a plastic bag and hidden in my
wardrobe. How you'd laugh if you knew. You wouldn't
understand, would you? Shakespeare would. Dante

would. All the great poets would understand. I love Jonathan Drake. I've loved him for over a year and I know he'll never notice me. Why should he? All the girls at school are in love with him. Except you. You only want his scalp to add to your collection, another heart to hang on that charm bracelet you keep jangling in front of my nose.

Rebecca did not, of course, say any of this aloud.

'Jonathan?' she asked, trying to sound uninterested. 'He's all right, I suppose. Bit conceited.'

'You can't really blame him. I mean, he's very good-looking. Don't you think so, Becky? Madge Hempson says he looks like a Greek god. Though I always thought Greeks were supposed to be dark, and he's so fair. Perhaps she meant a statue. Come to think of it, he is a bit like that photograph of the Apollo statue you've got hanging over your bed.'

'Is he? Can't say I've noticed,' Rebecca lied.

Why are you doing this to me, Cathy, she wondered silently? What have I done to make you want to hurt me? Is it because I got better exam results than you did? Or because I was chosen to be Juliet in the end-of-term play? Or does it go further back, to our first year at Braeside, when my drawing was pinned up on the art room wall and yours wasn't? Have you secretly resented me all these years?

'Please say you'll come, Becky,' Cathy said. 'It won't be the same without you. We've always done everything together . . .'

They had. Swimming together in the summer river, skating on the winter ice, eating peanuts side by side in the cheapest seats of the cinema, cycling over the switchback hills. Once the brakes on Rebecca's bicycle had gone and she'd hurtled down the hill helplessly towards the crossroads at the bottom. She'd survived then, with only a grazed knee and a buckled front wheel. Now she felt she was hurtling down a hill again, leaving her childhood far behind her, lost for ever. Her very memories were spoilt. It was like finding a maggot in an apple core: the taste of those years, once sweet, now made her want to vomit.

'Jonathan's calling for us at eight,' Cathy went on, taking her silence, if not for agreement, at least for a sign of weakening. 'You'll have plenty of time to wash your hair. We thought of driving out to that new place by the river. You know, The Green Willow. They say it's super. The food's good and there's a disco, and a riverside walk with coloured lights in the trees. And plenty of shadows, too,' she added with a little giggle that called up pictures of kisses in the dark. Cathy and Jonathan . . .

'I feel sick,' Rebecca said, 'in the back of a car.'

'You can sit in front. I don't mind.'

Rebecca stared at her. 'Who's driving, then?' she asked.

'Jonathan. It's his dad's car,' Cathy told her, her face as innocent as an angel's. 'I'll sit in the back with his friend.'

What was she up to? Was she so damn sure of Jonathan that she could condescend to be generous to her poor, lovesick friend? Just for half an hour's drive before she beckoned him away.

Oh Lord, thought Rebecca. Let me beat her at her own game. She stared hopelessly into the mirror. Eight o'clock. Plenty of time before then to have her hair dyed red, yellow or black, to have it cut short or brushed out into a flaming bush. Perhaps her mother would lend her the money to buy a new outfit: tight satin trousers or a swirling skirt. What did Jonathan like?

What he liked was sitting in front of her in a faded cotton dress from Marks and Spencers, with no need for make-up on her flower face, no hair-dye to dull the glowing lustre of her red-gold hair. No need for false eyelashes or fingernails, no padded bras to push her out or tight belts to hold her in. Cathy's puppy fat had all gone. She was a fully-grown bitch.

'We'll have fun, won't we?' she said.

'Yes,' Rebecca agreed, and thought about pushing her best friend into the river.

At seven o'clock that evening, Rebecca sat in front of her mirror, brushing her newly-washed hair. She had not had it dyed, nor had she bought anything new to wear. Why waste her money? Even if she had her hair dyed green, Jonathan probably would not notice.

Her mother would. Her mother noticed everything: a new lipstick, a pair of high-heeled shoes, a red silk shirt. Ever since Rebecca was fifteen, her mother had been watching her closely, dreading the day when her daughter would bring home a hideously unsuitable boyfriend, with long greasy hair and his shirt open to his navel.

'Where are you going this evening?' she'd ask, eyeing Rebecca's tight black trousers uneasily.

'To the cinema.'

'Who with?'

'Some friends from school.'

'Anyone I know?'

'Cathy, Sue, William – just the usual lot. No one in particular,' Rebecca would say, not mentioning Jonathan with whom she was already in love.

'Have a nice time, darling,' her mother would say, relieved.

Now that Rebecca was nearly seventeen, however, her mother's worries had changed.

'You're looking pretty tonight. Are you going out with anyone special?' she'd ask hopefully.

'Just Cathy.'

'Cathy's looking very glamorous nowadays, I must say. Has she got a boyfriend yet?'

'Yes. Several.'

'Oh well, there's safety in numbers,' her mother would say. 'Don't worry. You're very young still. Plenty of time to think of boyfriends when you've finished your exams. I'm glad you're so sensible.'

But her eyes would inspect Rebecca uneasily, as if wondering if there was anything wrong with this daughter who gave her no trouble; who never came home at three in the morning, or painted the walls of her room black and purple, or flounced out of the house in a screaming tantrum, vowing never to return. Who was so unlike the daughters of all her friends.

Poor Mum, Rebecca thought. It must be boring for her to have nothing to complain about at her coffee mornings. Perhaps I should have dyed my hair green for her sake – 'You'll never guess what Rebecca did! I could've screamed when I saw her. Her hair! Bright green!'

She smiled ruefully at her reflection. It was too late now. Light-brown hair, pale skin, hazel eyes. The face of a quiet, well-brought-up girl – as dull as ditchwater. Oh well, it was fitting. A second-best girl for a second-best boy. She wondered without much interest what he would be like. One thing you could bet on. He'd have spots.

He did. His name was Peter Swithin, and he had three ripe red spots on his chin. Otherwise he was unremarkable, of average height, skinny, with untidy dark hair, two strands of which hung over his spectacles like windscreen wipers. His eyes were on the small side but at least they looked at Rebecca when he was introduced to her, without showing any obvious sign of disappointment. Perhaps, she thought, he had expected worse.

She had had no faith in Cathy's promise that she could sit in the front seat of the car. She'd been sure that at the last moment Cathy would find a good reason why she herself should sit there. Rebecca was so astonished when Cathy climbed into the back without protest that she stood stupidly on the pavement, staring at the empty seat beside Jonathan.

'Come on,' he said. 'Or don't you trust my driving?'

She got in beside him, blushing and tongue-tied. She could think of nothing to say. She dared not even look at him for fear of seeing boredom or impatience on his face. Wishing she had never come, she sat stiffly in her seat, her elbows pressed tight against her sides, staring blindly in front of her as he drove through the outskirts of the little town. In the back seat, Cathy and Peter were whispering together, and she heard Cathy giggle.

Her cheeks flamed. She was sure that they were laughing at her. It would amuse Cathy to betray her secret to Peter. Oh Lord, had she told Jonathan as well? It was horribly easy to imagine. Perhaps she had said, 'Poor old Becky, she's hopelessly gone on you. You must've noticed, Johnny. She turns bright pink whenever she sees you. It's pathetic. You should've seen her face when I said she could sit next to you in the car. You don't mind, do you, Johnny? It's only till we get to The Green Willow, then we'll change partners.'

I hate her, Rebecca thought. Staring through the windscreen, she saw before her not the narrow winding road but a wide, shallow river, thick with mud and filth. She saw her best friend wallowing oozily out of it, her bright hair dimmed by a crown of scum . . .

And won't I laugh, she thought vindictively.

'. . . don't you agree?' Jonathan asked.

'Yes,' she said uneasily, having no idea what he'd been talking about.

'I wish Dad would get a new one,' he went on. 'This old rattle box has just about had it. And it's false economy, as I keep telling him. Everyone knows you should trade in a car every . . .'

Cathy giggled in the back again and the extra boy laughed. 'I don't believe you,' he said, 'you're making it up.' Then their voices sank to a low mumble again. Rebecca tried to turn round to glare at them, but the seat-belt and head-rest restricted her movements. All she got was a glimpse of two shadows sitting close together, and a crick in her neck.

'Do you know what I'd like?' Jonathan asked.

'No,' she replied truthfully, for she had not been listening to him, she was too busy trying to hear what they were saying behind her.

'A Range Rover,' he said. 'Does that surprise you?'

'Yes,' she replied. 'No. Perhaps.'

Fortunately he did not seem to expect her to take an intelligent part in his conversation, but went on to explain the reasons for his choice, talking with enthusiasm about engine capacity, speed ratio and petrol consumption.

'It's the four-wheel drive that appeals to me most,' he said.

'Yes. I can see that.'

'You can cross a desert in one, or go up a mountain –'

'A mountain?' Rebecca repeated blankly, for the countryside they were driving through was flat, with nothing higher than a hedge in sight.

'I don't mean Mount Everest, of course,' Jonathan said, taking his eyes off the road to smile at her briefly. 'But you could go quite a way up.'

'Yes, I suppose so.'

She must try and concentrate on what he was saying. This was Jonathan, whom she loved. And there she was, sitting beside him in the summer dusk, so close that their elbows nearly touched, and the air between them seemed to quiver. She turned her head and gazed admiringly at his profile. How beautiful he was, with the straight nose and rounded chin of an Apollo, and the close-fitting cap of dark-gold curls . . .

It's the happiest moment of my life, she told herself, or it would be, if only he'd shut up for a minute. I don't want to hear about cars. I want to hear what they're whispering about in the back, Cathy and the second-best boy. I bet they're planning to play some horrible joke on me.

She was wrong. They had no thought to spare for her, or for Jonathan, or for any of the chattering people at the little tables in the garden of The Green Willow. They did not look at them, but only at each other. Above their heads, a faded moon had risen and fairy lights flowered in the trees along the river bank. But nothing could outshine the brightness on their faces as they leaned together, eating chicken and chips out of the same basket. They were in love.

Good grief! Rebecca thought. What in Heaven's name can she see in *him*?

And she stared at Peter in astonishment, half-expecting him to have changed like the frog in a fairy tale. But he looked just the same as he had before, skinny and spotty and utterly unremarkable.

Was it a joke? Were they just pretending, play-acting in order to make a fool of her. No, Rebecca thought, seeing her friend's face glow like a pale flower in the moonlight, turning towards the spotted boy as if he were the sun. She watched them wander off hand in hand down the riverside walk, with the fairy lights high up in the trees and the kissing shadows below.

'I'm sorry if I'm boring you,' Jonathan said stiffly.

'What?'

'You haven't been listening to a word I've said, have you?'

'Yes, I have,' she said, adding quickly, before he could ask her to repeat his last sentence. 'Have you known Peter long?'

'Peter Swithen?' he asked, as if the world was full of Peters and he didn't much care for any of them. 'Yes. Ages. He's my cousin.'

'Is he very brilliant, or something?'

'No, not particularly. He's clever, but no cleverer than –' he hesitated. She was sure he'd been going to say "than me", but he changed it to 'Many other boys. Why?'

'I just wondered. Are his parents very rich?'

'Good Lord, no. His father's a teacher, and that's what he wants to be. Why all this interest in him? I must say it's rather the limit,' he added bitterly, 'when you ask a girl out, you don't expect her to do nothing but talk about your bloody cousin.'

'You didn't ask me. Cathy did,' Rebecca said, and smiled. She felt as if she had been given back the happy years of her childhood. There was no need to forget them now. Cathy had been a true friend all the time.

'Well, I knew you were coming,' Jonathan was saying. 'I mean, she asked you for me, didn't she? I can't see it makes any difference. I just don't understand you. I always thought you –' He broke off, with such a look of offended vanity on his face that she couldn't help laughing.

'You always thought I fancied you?' she asked mockingly; but then, seeing him flush and look hurt, she added kindly, 'Well, perhaps I do.'

As they walked hand in hand by the river, she glanced at him sideways. He was beautiful and clever, a little vain but you could hardly blame him for that. How odd of Cathy, she thought, to leave this treasure for me. Won't Mum be surprised when I bring him home. Won't all the other girls be sick with envy.

Yet she knew she would never feel for him again the same bitter-sweet adoration she had felt before. No longer would a single smile from him be enough to brighten a whole day. After all, if Cathy, who was so beautiful that she could have chosen any boy she wanted, had passed him over, it must mean that Jonathan was the second-best boy.

Rebecca was not certain whether to be glad or sorry. She had lost something. She did not belong any longer in the great company of tragic lovers, sighing for unattainable stars. This Romeo would be only too welcome at her house. He would probably talk to her father about cars . . .

But his hand in hers was warm and human. There was something to be said, she thought as she smiled at him, for second-best boys.

VIVIEN ALCOCK

Making Contact

She first saw the boy in Red Square. There was no snow yet, but it was bitterly cold with a hard bright sun that seemed to bite at her face with the same harshness as the cloakroom attendant in the Intourist Hotel, who had shouted at her when she had dumped her coat on him at the wrong time. That was the trouble with Moscow; you never knew the right time to do things.

He was with a group of Russian school children who were being shepherded across the square towards the golden domes of St Basil's Cathedral. Hanging back, he stared at her, seemingly with some kind of wonder. He was certainly good-looking, thought Jane, in a stocky, interesting Russian way. She supposed that he was about her own age, fourteen, or maybe a bit younger. As she watched, the boy slowly, unwillingly, walked away towards the cathedral. He was wearing a huge overcoat that seemed to swamp his small body, and with his shock of startling blond hair and a rosy complexion he looked frighteningly innocent.

'Today Red Square is 700 metres long and 130 metres wide.' Natasha, the Intourist guide, droned on and beside her, Sean yawned widely. They both disliked Natasha for

no particular reason except, of course, that she was com-
pellingly boring. Armed with enough statistics to give the
exact measurements of every public monument in the
Soviet Union if necessary, Natasha seemed to have a
deliberate policy of destroying any magical moment that
could have been achieved in a magical country.

Jane looked back to the boy. He was still there, still
staring at her. There was some kind of hold-up in his
group. The leader seemed to be having an argument with
an official who kept shrugging his shoulders at her.
Meanwhile, the children were reluctantly forming a
queue.

Natasha droned on. 'The Intercession Cathedral, also
known as St Basil's, is surely the jewel of Red Square.'

Immediately Jane wanted to argue childishly that it
wasn't. There was no doubt about it; the boy was still
staring at her. She wondered if Sean had noticed him.

'Now you will take photographs,' pronounced Natasha,
sweeping them all before her as if she was herding swine.

Then, quite suddenly, without her noticing, it
happened. The Russian boy was at her side. 'Meet me,' he
whispered. And to her amazement, he told her where.

Sean was fifteen and had been the boy next door all his life.
When Jane Atkins' father, a physicist, had been invited to
the Moscow State University to give some lectures her
mother decided to go too for moral support. She had
suggested taking Sean, but Professor Atkins had been
against the idea. 'Let her take a girlfriend,' he had advised.
'Sean's a blockhead and anyway I don't want any hanky
panky. Not at her age.' But Jane's mother had been
adamant. Sean came from a one-parent family. His father,
a truck driver, was on the dole and had Sean's three
younger brothers to look after as well.

'Give Sean the holiday of a lifetime,' she had urged her husband.

'But he's only interested in football and Jane – in that order,' returned Professor Atkins feebly, knowing that he had lost the argument before it had started. So Sean came and Jane was pleased. He was good company and wasn't just interested in football. He loved paintings and sculpture in a strange passionate way that Jane could not understand and he could not communicate, but he also had a great sense of humour and she very much enjoyed being with him. In the back of her mind she knew that he loved her as deeply as he loved his paintings, but as he could not talk about that either she chose to ignore it. She had lots of other boyfriends at home and none of them meant much to her. She did not want them to either.

Now they were sitting in the huge mausoleum-like foyer of the Intourist Hotel. Neither of them liked it very much and ever since they had come to Russia they longed to meet some Russians. But that had seemed impossible until now.

'We can't do it,' said Sean. 'Can we?'

'Why not?' asked Jane impatiently.

They both looked round the vast entrance hall with its bland videos and bustling tourists. This wasn't Russia. It was the tourists' cocoon. But now Russia had come to them. Someone was on their doorstep, making contact.

The swimming pool was the weirdest place they had ever seen. It was open air and plumes of steam rose from its surface, almost obscuring the walls of the Kremlin. They paused uncertainly at the entrance, sure now that they were making a big mistake and should not have come at all. They were bound to be wrong and, worse still, wrong in a Russian way. Also, it was not even clear which entrance they should use. Each was marked with a number and they stood miserably wondering who was going to be the first to suggest they should go back to the hotel. It was bound to be out of order to meet Russians in this way. Especially kids. They could be arrested and sent to Siberia.

'Hello.'

With a terrible jump they swung round. It was him. The boy.

'Have you brought your swimming things, like I said?'

They stared at him as wonderingly as he had stared at them in Red Square. They could not believe that he was actually here and speaking to them in rather stilted but near perfect English. Sean looked round him furtively as if the Secret Police were going to spring out on him at any moment.

'Well?' The boy looked at them impatiently. He was dressed as he had been the previous day, but somehow he looked even younger. He's probably a junior K.G.B. informer, thought Sean grimly, paid to trap tourists.

'Er – yes. We got 'em.' Sean felt totally inarticulate. But the boy was rushing forward. 'There is one place for the boys and another for the girls.'

'Not much different from England,' muttered Sean as he allowed himself to be hurried along.

But it *was* very different from England. The changing-rooms of the swimming bath had a nineteenth-century feeling to them. The walls inside were tiled and they were presided over by an old lady dressed in black. Jane, once the two boys had left her, felt particularly vulnerable. She had noticed these old ladies all over Moscow – on the Metro, sweeping the roads, clearing up the fallen leaves in the park. This one was quite friendly and with a series of grunts, nods and gestures showed Jane where to change, where to hang her clothes and how to have a shower before going into the water. Feeling rather tired, Jane then found herself walking down a tunnel. It was tiled again and very quiet and somehow rather sinister.

The boy did not say very much while they were changing, but he had an air of authority to him that Sean was slightly beginning to resent. 'What does he want?' Sean kept thinking. There must be something that he wants. When both boys had stripped down to their trunks Sean felt a sense of inferiority. He was tall for his age and muscular, yet when he looked at the Russian boy he saw that he was very compact for his small size. He was quick and neat in his movements and Sean wondered what kind of swimmer he was. That was Sean's weak spot. He could swim but he was not very powerful. Was the boy going to show him up?

'What's your name?' asked Sean almost aggressively as they both walked down the dank tunnel to the water. He shivered slightly, feeling almost chilled to the bone.

'Kolya,' replied the boy softly. 'My name is Kolya.'

'I'm Sean.'

'And what is your sister's name?'

'She's not my sister. She's my girlfriend.'

'But her name,' Kolya insisted, and Sean resented the authority in his voice. He was no longer scared and he felt an increasing hostility to the slim, lithe back in front of him.

'She's called Jane,' he snapped.

Both Jane and Sean forgot all their mixed and uneasy feelings about the Russian boy when they arrived in the pool. They had to climb down a ladder into the dark water, ducking under a kind of rubber flap before they got out of the tunnel, and with the tepid water lapping their shoulders they were filled with trepidation as they pushed their way out. But the outside was spellbinding. Clouds of steam partly hazed the Moscow skyline and it looked like a fairy tale city, ethereal with its domes and cupolas insubstantial in the mist.

The water was warm, almost the temperature of a bath, and their heads felt curiously icy. But once they plunged underneath the water, they were crisply warm again. It was the most odd feeling and made Jane suddenly almost lightheaded with joy. She felt as if she were literally on top of a strange and shimmering world, floating through the fantasy skyline of a forbidden and magical city. Sean was soon showing off as he often did with boys at home if she was around. She sighed. Trust Sean to ruin things. But Kolya did not seem to mind; he fought back, grabbing Sean's legs and pulling him under the water. Emerging, Sean grabbed him round the neck and Jane knew that the Russian boy was allowing Sean to duck him. Why?

Once Sean had succeeded in dominating Kolya, Jane noticed that his aggression was gone. Thank God for that. She had never felt so ecstatically happy in all her life.

'His name's Kolya,' said Sean.

'Pleased to meet you,' said Jane, instantly regretting the formality in her voice. She knew that Sean was laughing at her. But when she looked across at Kolya, his face was suddenly transfused with a warm smile. Immediately her joy returned, for the warmth made his rather alien innocence disappear and she felt she could know him now, that he was a person.

'Why did you want to see us?' she asked with a rush of confidence. Kolya paused and did not answer immediately and she wondered if some water had gone into his mouth.

Then he said abruptly: 'I want to know about England and
no one will tell me what I want to know.'

'But what do you want to know?' asked Sean very
sharply, too sharply for Jane, but Kolya did not seem to
notice.

'I want to know what it's really like and what people do
and how they think – and what they think of us out here.'

'But don't they tell you at school?'

Kolya did not reply at once. He looked around him
cautiously but almost casually as if it was something that he
was used to doing. Then he said: 'At school they don't tell
me what I want to know about England. They only tell me
what they think I should know.'

'Where do you go to school? What kind of school?' asked
Sean rather brusquely.

'To an English school.'

They both stared at him in amazement and Jane shivered.
'What do you mean – an English school?' she asked gently.

'If you are thought to be clever in this country you can go
to a school where every subject is taught in English. But they
still don't teach me what I want to know,' he added, 'and
that makes me really mad.' The Americanism touched Jane
and she suddenly realised that Kolya had a slight American
accent. It was somehow ironic.

'What do you want to know about England?' asked Sean
curiously.

'I want to know how English people really live and what
they do with themselves all day and all night. I want to
know if there are a lot of murders and I want to know what
is on your television. I also want to know exactly what
happens in the town of Bournemouth.'

'Bournemouth?' Sean was now looking at Kolya as if he
was completely mad and Jane felt a sudden urge to explode
in hysterical giggles.

'My father lives in Bournemouth,' he said and suddenly dived away from them, a translucent wraith under the misty water.

Immediately Jane experienced an agony of panic, feeling she had lost him for ever. And when he suddenly surfaced, the hard bright sun caught his glistening head. He looks like a little god, she thought idiotically. But the pain came and it would not go away, however much she tried. It was a sweet pain, a kind of tight band that was round her chest and her mind and her heart all at once.

Jane was swimming by herself now and the boys had moved away to play on the diving boards in a separate section of the pool. She turned again and again to look at Kolya and suddenly she longed to touch him as she had never touched anyone before. She wanted to jump into the diving pool and lock her legs and arms around Kolya's alien, silky, beautiful Russian body. She wanted to kiss his watery lips and to hold him close and never let him escape back into that anonymous wilderness of streets which would swallow him up and never return him to her. And all the time she was thinking about him, she was thinking that she was surprised to be thinking in this painful and extraordinary way. She also felt guilty because Sean had so much wanted to be as close to her as she wanted to be to Kolya, and she had never let him and indeed would never let him. Jane swam away from the boys and the desire that she felt she would always have with her now.

It all happened very quickly. In the changing-room Sean and Kolya had been larking around in the showers. Then they had been in adjoining cubicles, still messing around by flicking towels at each other. Eventually, too exhausted to speak, both boys had dressed, but when Sean had called out for Kolya he had not replied and when Sean looked for him he had not been there.

Disconsolately Sean searched the changing-rooms for him but there was absolutely no sign. Then he saw the other boys staring at him. Not like Kolya had stared at them in Red Square, but in a very hostile kind of way. They were staring at his clothes, and he was suddenly conscious of his well-cut Levis, sweater and leather jacket. But it was obvious that his clothes were not the main object of their gaze. There was something more. The leader of the group began to walk towards him. He was as tall as Sean, and gaunt, with a stride that Sean recognised all too well from home. The boy was holding a short-bladed knife.

Jane was changing in a state of mind that she had never felt before. She just did not know how to cope with her emotions. In one way she felt like bursting into song and in another she felt like dissolving into floods of tears. And all the time, the tight, painful band seemed to clutch at so many different parts of her at once. She changed quickly and rushed outside to meet the boys. But they were nowhere to be seen. For a while she waited patiently until it was well past the time of the Intourist hotel lunch and the first shades of worry began to seep into her mind. Where on earth could they have got to? Another five minutes passed and then another. Only one thought drummed at the threshold of her mind, flashing across as a terrifying slogan. Where was Kolya and what had he done to Sean?

A small sharp wind worried at the dead leaves around her and the domes of St Basil's flashed at her mockingly. Gone were their beauty and instead she saw a hard for-eignness that only wanted to exclude her, to laugh at her vain attempts to make sense of this mysterious country.

More minutes passed and her sense of panic grew. Then she wandered to the right of the great circular pool walls and saw a tiny, formal park. She saw a movement – or at least she thought she did. Relief flooded her. The boys were hiding from her. That must be what was going on. She smiled grimly. Russian or English, boys were all the same. They were just winding her up. The joy began to return to her and with it the painfully delicious band round her heart.

There was nobody else in the park, or at least that was what she thought at first; then she noticed a shelter in which two old men slept in the dusky sunlight like two fauns. She thought she saw the movement again in a tiny defile at the end of the park, beside a pile of old-fashioned gardeners' brooms. Those boys, she thought happily. Those stupid boys. She hurried forward, a smile playing on her lips.

Standing on top of the slope, Jane saw the mound move slightly and an idea flashed into her mind. She would go and jump on top of them. The thought filled her with a heady excitement. What would happen if she jumped on top of Kolya? Would he try and fight with her? What would she do if he did? With a wild cry, Jane ran down the slope and launched herself at the still slightly moving piles of leaves. 'You silly boys,' she screamed, and landed with a big thump on a soft warm body. She scrabbled away at the leaves but met with no resistance. Then she uncovered Sean's face. There was blood on his mouth and his forehead.

Jane could not believe what she was looking at. She began to cry and to tremble with the shock of what she had seen and she began to cry out his name, again and again. Slowly he sat up, his hand clasping the side of his head. 'Bastards,' he muttered.

After a while Sean was able to get to his feet and Jane led him over to a little iron bench where they both sat down. She looked over him carefully. Sean was cut and bruised; she could not see anything worse than that. But supposing there was – supposing he was hurt inside. They should go to a hospital. But if they did manage to find one, what on earth would they say? How could they make themselves understood?

Slowly, Sean told her what had happened. 'There was this very heavy guy who came up and I couldn't see Kolya anywhere. He pulled a knife and flashed it around but didn't use it.'

'But didn't anyone stop them?' she asked desperately.

'There was an old lady there.'

There always is, thought Jane grimly.

'But she was knitting. Anyway they all jumped me and started beating me up. I got a few back.' Sean paused reflectively. 'Then one of them got me in a half-nelson and they forced me outside.'

'But didn't you shout out? Try and attract someone's attention?'

'I was scared to. I mean – no one would have understood anyway and I might have been arrested. You never seem to see any trouble here in Moscow. I bet any problems are hustled away pretty quickly.'

'But where was Kolya?' Jane realised that she had not asked the most obvious question of all.

'That's the point. He'd scarpered. I was looking round for him when this lot showed up. Anyway they got me outside and there were people around but they looked away. Directly we got in the park we all started fighting and then they put me on the ground and I didn't know anything else until you turned up.'

Guiltily Jane decided against telling him that she had actually jumped on him.

'We should go to a doctor or a hospital or something . . .' Her voice trailed away.

'We'd never make ourselves understood. Anyway, I know I'm only bruised. Honest. I'll be all right.'

'Then we should go back to the hotel.'

'O.K.' Sean paused. 'But you'd better try and mop me up a bit first.'

Jane got out her hanky, spat on it and began to wipe at the fast congealing blood on Sean's face. As she rubbed, Jane looked around her, wondering if anyone had seen them. But the thought suddenly occurred to her that if a whole contingent of the Red Army marched into the park, they would avert their eyes and quickly disappear. For once they were away from Natasha, the hotel and the tours, they did not seem to exist. At least, not officially. She shivered. She so much wanted to belong, to have an identity here. She loved Russia, she knew she did. But as she continued to scrub away at Sean's face she realised that she was deceiving herself. She didn't love Russia. She loved Kolya.

In the Metro she looked at Sean's cut and bruised face and felt guilty. Dear Sean would die for her, she knew that. And all she could think about was Kolya. She took Sean's hand and squeezed it as they waited for the train, but he winced as she found his bruised knuckles. An instinct made Jane turn round and as she did so she stifled a scream.

Kolya was standing beside them.

Sean turned round and saw him. 'You little sod,' he began.

'Please to shut up.'

Sean's face was thunderous as he moved towards him

threateningly and Jane laid a restraining hand on his arm. As Kolya started to speak the train roared in. He looked around him and for the first time Jane read fear in his eyes.

'We cannot speak here. I want you to meet me.' He looked imploringly up at Jane.

'Where?' She was as frightened as he was now – it was a kind of raw, animal fear that you could almost smell.

'Which Intourist hotel are you at?' he hissed at her.

'The Cosmos.'

Kolya reacted with a smile of delight and Jane was captivated by its sudden charm. 'You turn left from your hotel. A few minutes away is a housing estate. You go to Block Nine. There is a playground in front. Meet me there tonight at seven.' He was gabbling now as the train doors slid open.

'What for?' asked Sean belligerently.

'To talk about Bournemouth,' said Kolya and immediately disappeared into the swarming crowd.

'We're not going.' Sean lay on the bed as Mr Gorbachev delivered strings of facts on the flickering television screen in his bedroom. 'Besides your parents are taking us to the Bolshoi tonight.'

'Then I'm going to have a sick headache.'

Sean sat up angrily. 'Don't be such a bloody fool. How can you even think of meeting him after that's happened. Wandering about at night amongst the housing estates. He isn't even to be trusted in daylight at a public swimming pool.'

'He's in trouble.' Jane knew that she was being senselessly obstinate. But she was obsessed with seeing him again, no matter what the dangers, and a strange sense of ruthlessness swept over her. Nothing mattered. Nobody mattered. Not Sean or her parents or anyone. Not even herself.

Sean looked at her curiously. 'Have you got a thing about this guy?'

'What?'

'You know – one of your things. Like you had a thing about Tommy Barton.'

'I never had a thing about Tommy Barton.'

'And then there was that boy on the fishing boat. And what about –'

'Why don't you shut up?' Jane suddenly hated him. Hated anyone who could get in her way, who could prevent her from seeing Kolya. She was going to him. Whatever happened. 'You go to the bloody ballet.'

'No way.'

'I can look after myself.'

'Sure.'

'So mind your own bloody business.'

'I'll tell your parents.'

'Tell them.'

'Jane.'

'Jane!' She mimicked him unmercifully. 'I'm going to him. He's in trouble.'

'You're in Russia.'

'So what?'

'They do things differently here. You'll get into big trouble.'

'A human being is in trouble, Sean. Can't you see that?'

Sean rubbed at his swollen mouth. Luckily it was going down a bit. He caught a glimpse of himself in the mirror. He didn't look too bad. Maybe the Atkins wouldn't notice and if they did he supposed he would have to say that he'd walked into a lamp-post. He tried again with Jane but he knew it was hopeless. He repeated: 'You've got one of your things.'

Jane threw a shoe at him.

Unfortunately for Sean, the Atkins believed in their
daughter's sick headache and they were grateful to him for
looking after her. Sean knew there was no stopping Jane
once she had an obsession – she was that kind of person.
As usual, however, he wondered why he was letting Jane
get away with it. 'You let those Atkins walk all over you,'
his dad had told him and he was quite right. He did. But
then he was in love with Jane and he knew he always
would be. Mostly he wished he could stop loving her but
that did no good. The fact of the matter was that he loved
her deeply – and always would love her that way. Sadly,
he knew that their future would always have Tommys and
Kolyas in it. Normally he would just ride it, but in this
case she was running herself headlong into danger in her
stubborn way. And he had to look after her. No matter
where she led him or what she did.

The housing estate was enormous. They could hardly
believe that there were so many high rise blocks. Jane
knew how selfish she was being, but she also knew she
was unable to stop herself as she careered on. But this
time, she told herself, it was different – different about
Kolya. Of course it was all absurd and incomprehensible,
but surely, Jane reasoned, that was what love was all
about. The guilt closed in on her again as Sean strode
watchfully by her side. Why did she use him so?

'Blimey.' Sean had halted suddenly in his tracks and Jane
came back to reality with a start. She looked up and
gasped. Brilliantly lit, the domed and cupolated church was
miniaturised by the towering blocks of flats around it.
Painted in blue and gold, the building looked outlandish
amongst its grey and uniform neighbours. Jane peered at
her watch. It was almost seven and she heard herself rather
brusquely telling Sean to hurry and look for Block Nine.

In fact it was just round the back of the church. And there was Kolya, standing under a lamp-post.

Directly he saw them, he signalled them over. Glancing round, he beckoned. 'This way.' He ran on and Sean hesitated, but Jane was beside herself.

'Come on! We'll lose him.' She ran after Kolya and with a sigh Sean followed her. Kolya ran into the darkened doorway of one of the flats and waited for them. Then, carefully checking around him he ran up a flight of concrete steps with Jane and Sean close behind him. They came to a door, Kolya pushed at it and it creaked open. He signalled them in. Sean stiffened. The place was in pitch darkness. What kind of trap was this?

Kolya lit a candle and when they looked round they found they were standing in an empty flat with some sacking on the floor and a few battered cushions. It was extremely cold and Jane shivered miserably as Sean put an arm around her protectively. 'Yes,' said Kolya, 'this is not a very comfortable place.'

'You're dead right,' said Sean. 'Now what the hell do you want with us?' His lip was hurting again and he felt desperately tired. He stared at Kolya hard and reckoned he could handle him, but hoped he would not have to. He had done enough fighting for one day.

'I am very sorry that you were hurt. It was Oleg's doing really. They are animals. At least they are when they are on the defensive.'

'Defensive? You could have fooled me!' said Sean with derision.

Kolya smiled a slow smile. 'They are good friends. They were trying to protect me.'

'Protect you?' Jane stared at him while Sean shrugged his shoulders angrily. Who did they think they were, these bloody silly Russians? But Jane was determined to seek some clarity.

'What have we done to you? And why do you want to know about Bournemouth?'

'You have done nothing to me and I am very sorry. It was I who approached you. Please forgive me.' He paused and then said with eyes brimfull of a strange kind of desire. 'Please help me.'

'But how?' asked Jane with desperation. 'How can we help you?'

'Tell me about Bournemouth.'

'Oh not Bournemouth again,' said Sean scornfully.

'Now you shut your useless mouth.'

'Right,' said Sean. 'I've had enough.' But he made no movement forward and Kolya immediately added contritely: 'I'm very sorry. Again. You see – you must understand that my father . . . It is he who lives in Bournemouth.'

'Yes,' said Sean. 'We know that. But we want to know why.'

'It is really quite simple. My father is a writer. He was a great writer here. A novelist. A master storyteller. But he wrote other things, things that were secret and not for publication. Things that were against the government. He was at a conference in your country when he had the news that they had found his other writing. He knew that he could not come back. Or at least if he did he would not be allowed to live with us any longer. So he chose to stay.'

'You mean he defected?'

Kolya shrugged. 'You have different words than us. He stayed. He has friends in your country. And he hopes that we will be able to join him. Me and my sister and my mother. He is working towards that every day of his life. I know that. But I also know that they are not going to let us go.'

'So he lives in Bournemouth?'

'Yes. He lives there. And no one will tell me about Bournemouth. No one.' Kolya began to cry. His whole body trembled with great hard wracking sobs. Of tears, there was no sign.

'Listen, you stupid herbert,' said Sean. 'It so happens that I've been to Bournemouth more times than you've had hot dinners.' Kolya looked at him blankly.

'Have you?' asked Jane suspiciously.

'Yes.' Sean gave her a rather nasty smile. 'It so happens that when Dad had a job, back in the dark ages when he was driving the truck, one of his main journeys was down to Bournemouth. I haven't been there for a couple of years but I remember it very well. So bloody listen.' Sean went over to Kolya and pushed him down on one of the cushions. Then he sat down beside him and put his arm around his shoulders. 'Now listen and listen good because I'm not going to the trouble of repeating myself.' He looked up at a hypnotised Jane. 'And you – you sit down and listen too.' Obediently she sat down.

'Now,' said Sean. 'Directly you come into Bournemouth . . .' For the next hour Sean told Kolya every possible detail he could remember about Bournemouth. And Kolya listened with all the wondrous attention of a young child being read the finest and most riveting story of his life. It was only when Sean was winding up about the chines that led down to the beach that they heard the noise on the stairway.

They were all rooted to the spot. The absurd phrase kept drumming over and over again in Jane's terrified mind. This it, thought Sean. Enter the K.G.B.

The door opened slowly. They'll be wearing hats, thought Sean. The K.G.B. always wear hats. But instead a boy crept into the room and Sean almost laughed aloud in relief. Then he tensed in anger. It was the boy who had headed the attack on him. But before anything could happen Oleg rushed across to Kolya and began to whisper at him in urgent Russian.

Sean realised he still had a protective arm around him and that Oleg had not questioned that at all. Slowly he took it away and Kolya stood up. His small, stocky, neat frame was shaking all over and his blond hair looked like rats' tails in the half light.

'I have to go,' he said. 'I have to go now.' His eyes were dead.

'Why?' asked Jane.

'They are taking my mother away.'

'Who?'

He gazed hopelessly at them. 'They are taking my mother away. You must not come.'

'Rubbish,' said Jane and went to the door. But she was blocked by Oleg. 'Get out of my way,' she said. But Oleg had a familiar object in his hand. A short-bladed knife.

Kolya pushed past them as Oleg raised his knife menacingly. Then he turned away and both Russian boys were racing down the stairs. As Jane hurried to follow them, Sean clutched at her and found he was gripping thin air.

'You can't get mixed up in this,' he yelled after her retreating back. The answer drifted back up the stairwell:

'Get stuffed.'

But Jane was not to get very far. Sean found her staring about in the darkness.

'I can't see where they've gone,' she wailed, looking so upset that Sean threw his arms round her and kissed her. '*You're* good at cuddling people tonight,' she said sourly.

They began to search the estate, he aimlessly and she desperately. Each darkened avenue between the blocks looked the same. Jane was beside herself and was sobbing

as hard as Kolya had. The church loomed up in front of
them again, its bright light spilling out into the darkness.

'Let's see if he's in there.'

'Why should he be?' asked Sean.

They walked in and he was.

The inside of the Russian Orthodox Church was
dazzling in its splendour and after the grey streets it came
as a sharp and majestic contrast. Sean was surprised. He
had always thought religion was banned in Russia. Jane
nudged him and pointed. Kolya was sprawled in
supplication on the floor. There were others with him,
mainly old people, and for a moment they thought that he
was the only child in the whole building. Then they saw
Oleg coming out of the shadows and making for them.

'Don't start anything in here,' Jane hissed at him but
Sean was too tired to react. He nodded dumbly.

To their considerable surprise, Oleg came up to them
and spoke in English. It was as good as Kolya's. Pity he
didn't use it before, thought Sean. We might have got on
better.

'You must not disturb him,' said Oleg softly but his
eyes were looking away from them.

'His mother,' hissed Jane. 'He said that they had taken
away his mother.'

'That is true.'

'But what will they do with her?'

'Help her.'

'Re-educate her?' snapped Jane.

'You are so stupid with your prejudices that you –' Oleg
seemed at a loss to know how to continue in English.
Then he recovered himself. 'You must understand a
private matter. Kolya's father is travelling abroad on business and his mother has regrettably been taken ill. In fact I
could tell you that she has a social problem. A problem

connected with alcohol. A great many people have suffered from this problem but now our government is – is dealing with the difficulty. She has been taken to a good hospital where specialists will help her.'

Jane was certain that he was lying but Sean was not so sure. He hoped that Jane was not going to be stupid.

'I don't believe you,' she said baldly. Sean tensed but Oleg merely shrugged.

'I'm not interested in whether you believing me or not.'

'Where will he live – now his Mother has been taken away?' she asked icily.

'Until she comes out of hospital, Kolya will be living with his grandmother.'

Jane stared down at the still recumbent Kolya and there was a long silence between them. Oleg broke it sourly. 'It is not a habit that his friends are pleased that he has acquired but his father was a religious man.'

'Was?' asked Sean.

Oleg grinned. 'Forgive me – I muddle your tenses.' For a moment he seemed more relaxed, but Sean turned on him sullenly and whispered:

'Do you expect me to forgive you for giving me a beating this morning?'

'We were acting in Kolya's interests.'

'How do you figure that out?'

'Our friend Kolya behaved stupidly. Naturally he misses his father when he travels abroad – it is understandable.' Oleg paused and then sunk his voice to an angry whisper. 'And you are simply interfering tourists who have been taught to think bad things about the Russians by your own capitalist society as well as the Americans.'

'Bollocks!' said Sean but Oleg merely looked puzzled.

'You had no right to attack Sean,' said Jane, but he

noticed sadly that there was no energy in her voice. She walked over to Kolya.

'It is not permitted to fraternise with foreigners in this way and our security people would be very alarmed. It could be very hard for Kolya – you too. You could be punished far more than you were.' He tried to break away from Sean and walk towards Kolya and Jane who were moving slowly towards a little side chapel. Sean laid a hand on Oleg's arm.

'Let them talk. There can be no harm in that.'

'There is harm. I have to look after him,' he muttered as if to himself.

'Yes,' whispered Sean. 'And I have to look after her too.' Oleg nodded. Awkwardly they stood together as a priest began to chant.

The chapel was completely deserted and they sat in a small recess behind a cluster of burning candles. Jane put her arms around Kolya and kissed him full on the lips. He tried to say something but she whispered: 'Don't let's talk. Don't ever let's talk.' And they didn't.

After a while Jane could feel Kolya's arms going around her. He feels lovely, she thought. And he smells lovely too. He smells of Moscow. Of fog and water and incense and beeswax and foreignness. They sat for minutes, cuddling each other. Then she felt his cold lips on her face and at last on her own. She buried her face in his big overcoat and wept tears of joy and pain. When she looked up she could see that he was doing the same.

Eventually Jane knew that she would have to break the spell. Very gently she disentangled herself from Kolya and for a moment she could feel him resisting, hanging on to her with a sudden strength that she did not know he possessed. Then, just as suddenly, he let her go. She clasped his hand as they stood up and they walked across the mosaic floor of the little chapel very slowly. As they walked Jane had the odd sensation that they were walking over miles and miles of land. Then, as they rounded the corner into the main church, they simultaneously loosened their grasp and Jane almost laughed aloud. At the same time she had the feeling that Kolya was laughing too.

Sean and Oleg had buried their hostility and were talking about football. Seeing them Oleg hurried up to Kolya and whispered to him in Russian. Kolya then turned to Jane.

'I have to go to my grandmother's now,' he said.

'Can't we go with you and meet her?' asked Jane eagerly.

'No,' said Oleg and Sean almost in unison.

Jane looked appealingly at Kolya but he shook his head.

'She is a very old lady. She would not be able to understand all the – implications. It would not be right to expect her to.'

'But how can I see you again?'

'Don't forget we go home tomorrow,' said Sean bleakly and Jane glared at him as if she could kill him. He winced visibly and Oleg permitted himself a smile.

Kolya shook his head. 'I must go to my mother in the early morning and then there is school . . .' His voice tailed away.

'And the flight leaves in the afternoon,' put in Sean but this time Jane showed no mercy as she turned on him.

'Why don't you just shut up?'

Sean scowled as Oleg said:

'Your friend is the voice of reality.'

'Will you ever come back?' Kolya's voice was desolate.

'Oh yes,' said Jane in a rush of words.

'You'll need a visa,' said Oleg. He seemed united with Sean in a mutual grim reality. Jane hated them both.

'I'll get one, you'll see,' she snapped childishly. She turned back to Kolya. 'Will you wait for me?' she asked as Sean with childish derision played an imaginary violin behind her and Oleg permitted himself another of his reluctant smiles.

'Yes,' said Kolya. 'I'll wait.'

'But where shall I find you?' asked Jane in sudden despair. Even she was now realising the enormity of the task she had set herself. 'I could write if you give me your address.'

Kolya shook his head. 'It will take you time to make the arrangements,' he said eventually.

'Like forever,' said Sean bitterly. Perhaps the 'thing' would pass. After all, the others had. Hadn't they?

'When can we meet?' asked Jane.

Kolya paused. Then he said, with sudden decision, 'In a year today.'

'Where?'

'On the Lenin Hills, by the University. There is a little church. We shall meet outside it. I shall be there alone. And that is a promise.' He looked very hard into Jane's eyes and then gave a signal to Oleg. Both boys ran out of the church without a backward glance, leaving Sean and Jane staring hopelessly after them.

So distracted were they, that Jane and Sean walked slowly away in the wrong direction. Sean was worried. He had never seen her so unhappy and definitely this was one of her bigger things – if not the biggest. He was afraid to speak to her for anything he said would be quite inadequate. So they strode on in the biting wind, dead leaves rising to swirl in the icy gusts. There seemed to be hardly anyone around and when he looked at his watch he saw that it was almost midnight. He suddenly realised with horror that Jane's parents would have returned from the ballet and were no doubt causing diplomatic hell in the Intourist hotel at this very moment.

Just as he was about to cut into her thoughts and say that they must find the hotel without delay, they came out on to a large road that was entirely unfamiliar.

It was very wide, very deserted. The wind had dropped and there was a great, cold stillness that seemed almost a brooding force surrounding them. Sean was reminded of all Russia stretching away from him. Then he grabbed at Jane's arm, pulling her back into the shadows. A police convoy was coming up the road, sirens blaring.

The lights of the convoy disappeared, swallowed up in a final darkness and Jane and Sean began to retreat into the estate again, trying to find the way back to the hotel. This time they went hand in hand, but Sean somehow knew that nothing would ever be the same between them again.

They stood on the Lenin Hills overlooking the whole of Moscow. The morning was bright and sunny and cold. There had been the kind of row that Sean had predicted last night when they finally got back to the hotel, but their story, weak as it was, came to be believed after a lot of argument as they had clung to it through thick and thin. The claim was that Jane had recovered sufficiently to take a late walk and, accompanied by Sean, had tried to clear her head in the moonlight. Inevitably it was Sean who took the flak, but now as they stood on the wide pavement in the icy brightness, Sean knew that he had lost her, would always be condemned to be the boy next door.

Jane looked down at the vastness of the city. Somewhere, amongst those thousands of patient Russians in the streets was Kolya. She turned back to the small church behind them. There was a bride and groom waiting to go in. 'Look – there's a wedding.' But Sean did not want to look and Jane's gaze returned to the strands of mist rising from the shining building. She knew how cruel she was being to Sean – knew she would go on being cruel to him for she could not help herself. Then Kolya's face swam into her consciousness. Next year, she whispered inside herself. Next year in Moscow.

ANTHONY MASTERS

The Triumph of Love

None of us had to be told why Alice Harlaw had taken to visiting our mother in the middle of university term. We – my three sisters and I – all knew that people didn't visit our mother at unusual times unless they were in trouble. But the point was, what kind of trouble could a quiet, steady girl like Alice Harlaw have fallen into?

Certainly, we agreed, it wasn't likely she had much of a home life; not with a father who was the minister of our local Presbyterian church and who – for good reason – the village had nicknamed 'Holy Willie'. But what did she have to bother her apart from that? She was well into her first year of medicine at Edinburgh University; and, so we'd heard, was enjoying her studies. We didn't think, either, that she lacked for boyfriends, because she wasn't at all a bad-looking girl –

'*If* you like sandy hair and freckles.' Helen, the oldest of us, summed up this part of our argument, and looked complacently at our bedroom mirror for the reflection of her own dark locks and clear complexion.

'You're just jealous,' Lillian said, 'because Alice is clever, and you're a dummy.' Lillian liked clever people because she herself was brainy; and although she was also quiet, as a rule, she could still always bring any of us down to earth.

'We'll see who's a dummy!' Helen retorted; and we all knew what to expect then. It was true that Helen didn't have what our teachers called 'an academic mind'. But she was cunning, and she was also an expert eavesdropper, so that it didn't take *her* long to learn what was bothering Alice Harlaw.

'She wants to get married,' Helen reported back to us. 'And her da won't let her.'

Married? At eighteen, and still only in her first year at University? In silence we chewed over the obvious question this raised, and I duly cleared the way for it to be asked.

'George!' I ordered our small brother. 'Go out to play, George.'

Reluctantly, George rose. 'Girls!' he said scornfully, and kept his dignity by sauntering out as slowly as he dared. Helen made sure he wasn't listening at the keyhole, then turned to shake her head at us and say:

'No, she doesn't *have* to get married. She's not – you know – "expecting".'

'Then why?' Lillian demanded. 'What's so wonderful about getting married when she could be studying medicine?'

That was Lillian's own dearest wish – to study medicine. But we all knew she didn't have much chance of her wish being granted – not with our mother trying to manage on a widow's pension and the little bit she could earn until we were old enough to leave school and get some kind of a job – *any* kind, so long as it would help out with the money. And now here was Alice chucking up the very career that Lillian would have given anything to have! Elinor rushed into the awkward silence that had fallen on us.

'Um – er – this fellow Alice wants to marry. Does he

belong to a different church from her dad? And is *that*
what's bothering Holy Willie?' Lillian and I followed her
expectant look at Helen, because we'd had experience of
that kind of thing in our own family and knew the ructions
it could cause. Helen drew a deep breath, and rolled her
eyes dramatically. Helen always *loved* being dramatic; and
in hushed tones now, she announced:

'It's worse, much worse than anything you could imagine in that line. Alice's fellow is an Indian. And he's a
Hindu!'

It took us a moment or two to recover from the shock of
this. Then there was a lot of confused questioning and
accusations about Helen just making things up – as usual –
before we finally established all the facts of the case.

The man Alice wanted to marry, it seemed, *was* an
Indian, by the name of Rajev; and he, too, was in first-year
medicine at Edinburgh University. There was no doubt,
either, that he was a Hindu – Helen swore she had clearly
heard Alice tell our mother so; and Helen, this time, didn't
use any of her dramatic tricks, so that we were quite sure
she hadn't made *that* up. We believed her too, when she
said that his family was one of those posh ones that Hindus
call 'high caste'. But it was a different matter altogether
when she rolled her eyes again before she finished:

'And just imagine! He pays his university fees in
diamonds.'

We yelled with derision at this, and Elinor began
driving the insult home with her famous imitation of Mrs
Knox – an old harridan we all disliked and who happened
to own a circlet of rhinestones that she always referred to
as 'my diamond tiara'.

'Ooh, my terara!' Elinor squawked; and immediately
became Mrs Knox hobbling into the annual Golf Club
dinner-dance, clutching the faded satin of her long gown

in one hand and steadying the circlet of rhinestones with the other. 'Ooh, my diamond terara!'

You could really see and hear Mrs Knox there in the room, as she did this; and so it was no wonder Lillian and I fell about laughing at her. But Helen, of course, didn't laugh. She screamed with rage, in fact, and made a dive at Elinor; but Lillian and I pulled her off, and there was quite a fight then until we had finally made her admit to the real truth about Rajev's diamonds – which wasn't at all spectacular the way *she* would have liked it to be.

All there was to tell, in fact, was that he had earned a commission on the sale of some diamonds for a relative in India, and had used the money to pay his fees. But once we'd got all that straightened out and Helen had stopped sulking over being robbed of her bit of drama, it wasn't long before we all got back again to the nub of the whole situation – which was simply this.

Alice's father, the Reverend Daniel Harlaw, was one of those ministers who really deserved the nickname of 'Holy Willie'. He was smooth, he was unctuous, he wore his religion like a well-pressed suit of clothes. *But*, underneath that smooth surface was an iron man who got his own way in everything. What was more, he was a snob who looked down his nose at everyone who wasn't of his class and his colour – and Alice was his pride, his joy, the one and only light of his narrow life. Poor Alice! That girl, we were all finally agreed, seemed to have as much chance of being allowed to marry her Rajev as she had of lighting a candle from the moon!

'And so you'll just have to listen again,' the rest of us told Helen. 'Because we *must* find out what she's planning to do now.' Helen looked smug, and even smugger when she came back with the next bit of news.

'Alice,' she reported, '*doesn't* want to give up her

studies. What she and Rajev have planned, in fact, is for each of them to take their degree. Then she'll go back with him to India; and they'll work together there as doctors, among the poor people of Rajev's home town.'

Lillian's face had lit up with admiration as she listened to this. But Elinor, practical Elinor, immediately demanded:

'And how much does Holy Willie know about this wonderful plan?'

'The lot,' Helen told us. 'And what's worse, it looks as if he's managed to ruin it.' Very soberly for her, then, Helen went on, 'Rajev took the bus down from Edinburgh to tell Mr Harlaw all about it, and to ask his permission to marry Alice. Harlaw threw him out on his ear. Then he went up to Edinburgh, saw the Chancellor of the University, and cancelled Alice's enrolment. That's why she's at home now, with so much time to come and talk to Mam.'

We were all very sober after that, with all of us suddenly seeming to realise the kind of questions that had never previously occurred to us. How could Alice tell whether or not she was truly in love with Rajev? And if she wasn't truly in love, wouldn't she be better to give him up rather than have her career ruined? Besides which, could a mixed marriage really work? Not that *we* knew anything about mixed marriages, or about being in love either, for that matter of it. Four girls still only in our early teens – how could we know?

Somehow or other, all the same, we still felt we had to talk about it – maybe because we were really concerned about Alice now, instead of just being curious about her. Maybe too, it was just because we *were* so concerned that Helen became less careful than usual in her eavesdropping. And that was how the balloon eventually went up for all of us, when she was caught listening-in on the night of Alice's next visit.

It took quite a while to get things sorted out that night, what with our mother being so mad at us and Alice being so upset. We had to admit to everything we knew, and then swear on the Bible that we'd never reveal it to a soul in the village; but once all that was over, our mother spoke in a way that surprised all of us – including Alice.

'Well now, Alice, the girls are suitably ashamed of the way they've behaved, and so what d'you think of letting them stay to hear your problem being discussed sensibly, for a change? You can't take the knowledge of it out of their heads, after all. And who knows, the questions they might have to ask could be the very ones to let light into your own mind. Into theirs, too, some day in the not-too-distant future – because you're not really all that much older than them, are you?'

'W-e-ell . . .' Alice wasn't sure about this suggestion, but she didn't actually raise any objections to it. We had, after all, taken our Bible-oath not to broadcast her story; and so we all sat down and looked primly at her until Elinor (trust Elinor!) summoned the nerve to ask cheekily:

'Will you wear a sari, Alice, when you're in India?'

We would all have laughed at this – even Alice, I think, would have laughed if Lillian hadn't immediately said in a tragic voice:

'If she ever gets to India. If she ever gets to *be* a doctor.'

Alice was puzzled for a moment by this, then her face cleared. 'Oh!' she exclaimed. 'You're bothered about me not being able to get a place at Medical School in some other university!'

Lillian nodded, and said unhappily, 'You and Rajev both.'

'It won't be easy,' Alice admitted. 'But we'll have help, you know, because they weren't at all pleased at Edinburgh when my father stopped my course there. The

Chancellor was furious about that, in fact, and he's told
me since that he'll back my application to any other university in the world – if that's what I want. *And* he said, if
Rajev and I got married, and wanted to study together,
he'll back Rajev's application too.'

'You're lucky,' Lillian said; and it was really sad to hear
the envy in her voice then. 'But how will you pay for it all?
I mean, travel, fees, and all that?'

Alice smiled at her. 'Money won't be a worry. Rajev's
an only son, you see, and he inherited everything in his
father's estate – which doesn't make him rich, of course.
But I think you could still say he's a reasonably well–off
man.'

'He's also a black man.' Helen spoke in a loud and
suddenly harsh voice, her face turning scarlet with a surge
of some sort of feeling we'd never guessed at before. 'How
can you even think of marrying a black man?'

'Rajev's not black.' Alice looked more bewildered than
upset by Helen's outburst. Then suddenly she too went
red in the face, so red you couldn't even see her freckles.
'Rajev's an Indian,' she said furiously. 'He's – he's a – a
sort of brown colour. But anyway, I'd love him still, even
if he was black as your own coalhole, Miss Helen
Blabbermouth.'

Our mother opened the Bible she had produced for our
oath. She began reading from it, lines I recognised from
The Song of Solomon.

'*I am black, but comely. Look not upon me because I am*
black, because the sun hath burned me. Set me as a seal upon
thine heart, as a seal upon thine arm; for love is as strong as
death.'

Nobody spoke when our mother had finished reading.
Nobody moved. She looked at Helen and said quietly:

'One thing that love is *not*, Helen. Love is not skin–deep.

You will apologize to Alice.' Helen muttered her apology, which Alice took rather sulkily, until our mother said to her, 'I'm afraid you'll have to look on Helen's youth as the excuse for her being so hurtful to you. But if you do marry Rajev, my dear, I'm afraid also that it's the kind of hurt you'll encounter all too often from others who don't have even that excuse.'

Alice's chin came up with a defiance I'd never seen in her before. 'In that case,' she said grimly, 'I'll just have to learn to live with it, won't I?'

'You'll have to learn to live with a lot of things,' our mother pointed out. 'The differences between your two races, your two cultures —'

'I'm not stupid,' Alice interrupted. 'And neither is Rajev. We've discussed all that, and —'

'And your two religions.' Relentlessly, our mother pursued her theme. 'You were brought up a Christian, Alice; and the question is, will you sacrifice that, too, for love?'

'It's not a question I'll have to answer,' Alice told her. 'Rajev and I have no intention of trying to change one another.'

Our mother heaved a sigh of relief. 'Parents, then,' she said. 'I know that Rajev's mother and your own mother hold the same view — they just want you young people to be happy. But your father, Alice! You know as well as we do that there never was a more unyielding man; and so you must know, too, dearie, what will happen if you *do* marry Rajev. You'll never see your father again. And can you accept that, Alice? Can you?'

To our utter astonishment, then, Alice Harlaw bowed her sandy head and wept. I mean to say — weeping because she'd never see Holy Willie again! In other circumstances, I suppose, we would have had quite a giggle over the idea. But none of us felt like laughing then — not with Alice sobbing about what a good daddy he'd always been to her, and how she knew it would break his heart if she went off with Rajev, and it was breaking *her* heart now to think of the way he would grieve for her.

We were a bit sniffy ourselves by the time she'd finished. To my own surprise, in fact, I was feeling a twinge of sympathy even for Holy Willie! Our mother let Alice have her cry out; and then, very gently, she asked:

'Well, Alice? *Can* you accept it?'

'I don't know,' Alice said miserably. 'Not yet, anyway. Not just yet.' And it was not until her next visit that Alice did make up her mind – or, rather, that she had it made up for her.

Rajev was with her on this next occasion. He'd come from Edinburgh on the bus, and hung about in the evening darkness till he'd spotted her cycling down the road from the manse. They'd stood talking for a few minutes, then he'd walked along to our house with her – and were we thrilled when he bowed to us, putting the palms of his hands together in front of him the way Indians do! Nothing like this had ever happened to *us* before. I saw the gleam that came into Elinor's eyes, and guessed it wouldn't be long before she added an Indian greeting to her repertoire of imitations!

I could only gape at him, this small and slender man with his glossy black hair and eyes of such lustrous brown, and think what an exotic-looking creature he was. But then Alice took him to sit close beside her on the sofa, and you didn't have to be told how much they were in love with one another – not with the feeling you got from them then. There was a sort of completeness about them together, a oneness that seemed to isolate them from the rest of us – as if, it suddenly occurred to me, they knew that all they would *ever* need was each other.

I wondered if all couples who were in love gave off the

feeling I was getting from Alice and Rajev; if that was
what was meant when it was said that two people were
'made for each other'. Then I began to wonder when the
polite conversation would be over so that we could get
down to the real talking – and had the answer to this
sooner than I expected. It came from George, wandering
in from his nightly diversion of hanging about by the
bright light of the village chip-van, a bag of chips in his
hand, and the smell of vinegar wafting from him.

'Hey!' George's eyes had gone immediately to Alice.
'Your dad's looking for you. And is he mad! He knows
you've got that darkie with you.'

'What?' Our mother pounced on George, outraged by
the word 'darkie', but still determined to shake even more
information out of him; and in short order then, she had
discovered everything he knew.

Somebody, it seemed, had seen Alice and Rajev
standing talking together and had hared straight up to the
manse to warn the minister of the scandalous company
being kept by his daughter. Holy Willie had dashed out
immediately to drag Alice home; but she and Rajev, of
course, had gone from their meeting-place by then. And
so now her father was scouring the village for her,
knocking at doors, searching every alley and dark corner –

'And carrying on something *terrible!*' George finished
with a relish that almost earned him another shaking.

'You've got to get away,' Alice cried in panic to Rajev.
'You've got to run, Rajev!'

'Not without you,' Rajev told her. 'And if we go
together this time, Alice, it's for good.'

I suppose the silence that followed this could have lasted
for only a few seconds; but to me at least, it seemed to go
on and on and not to be a silence at all but simply an
emptiness that echoed with our mother's voice asking *Can*

you accept that, Alice? and Alice's voice saying *don't know,
don't know, don't know* . . . Alice and Rajev were standing
close together, hands clasped, eyes searching one another's
faces.

'I'll go with you,' Alice whispered at last. 'For good this
time, Rajev. For good.'

'Well!' our mother exclaimed. 'If *that's* your decision,
the first thing to do is to make sure your father doesn't find
you here.' Quickly she turned to Lillian. 'Lillian, get
Alice's bike away from our gate. Ride it back to the
manse, but don't let Mr Harlaw see you on it. Go the back
way, through Baker's Wood.'

Lillian had begun to shake, and now she protested, 'But
I can't, Mam. It's spooky in Baker's Wood. And I'm
scared of that place. You know I am.'

'Yes, I do know, but –' Gently our mother cupped
Lillian's face between the palms of her hands. 'Dearie,' she
asked, 'what about Alice's career?'

The question was the only one that could have struck
the spark that lit a flame of courage in our timid Lillian.
Off she went, pale-faced still, but with a new look of
determination on her; and our mother turned then to
Helen.

'Now you,' she said. 'I've put up with plenty in my time
with you pretending to faint so you could get my
sympathy. But you're quite good at the acting and so
that's how you'll have to gain us time to think of a way of
getting Alice and Rajev to the bus-stop without Alice's
father catching her. Away and find Mr Harlaw, then pretend to faint or throw a fit in front of him. Be as daft as
you like, so long as you hold him up for a while at least.'
Helen was off in the instant, eyes gleaming at the prospect
of acting it up in front of Mr Harlaw – maybe even in front
of the whole village!

'But that still mightn't hold him for long enough,' our mother worried; and turned to Elinor. 'Elinor, can you imitate Rajev's voice?'

Elinor grinned, a great wide cat's grin of delight. 'Mr Harlaw!' she called. 'Are you looking for me? I am Rajev, the dark gentleman from India who wishes to marry your oh-so-white daughter!'

It was wickedly clever of her, the way she caught exactly the pitch of Rajev's voice as well as its intonation! And not only that, but also the way she had guessed at the very form of words that would infuriate Holy Willie enough to turn aside from his hunt for Alice to search for Rajev instead – which, of course, was exactly the trick our mother had intended her to play.

'But remember, Miss Clever,' she warned Elinor, 'he'll need only one glimpse of you to connect you with that voice, so be sure to keep to all the very darkest corners when you're shouting around the village.'

Elinor grinned again and skipped out, singing the words of a playground game we used to play when we were small – *Ye canna catch me, for a big bumbee* . . . I came at last to a decision in the fierce struggle I had been having with my conscience, and blurted out:

'Mam, you don't have to worry any more about how to get them out of the village. I can do that.'

Our mother, Alice, Rajev, all turned to stare at me. Their voices came in chorus. '*You* can?'

'I know a way to the bus-stop beyond the village – the one at Redhouse Castle; a way that means Mr Harlaw won't see them because it doesn't run through the village. I can show it to them – if George stands shot for me at the foot of the garden, that is.'

George jumped to his feet, eager to take part at last in all this unexpected excitement. Our mother stared even harder at me.

'And why didn't you tell us this before?'

I hated having to answer her. I was giving up enough, wasn't I, without having to make excuses for not being quicker to make my sacrifice? I looked away from her, and muttered:

'Because it was *my* secret. And I just didn't want to give up my secret to anybody.'

Our mother turned back to Alice and Rajev. 'She never tells lies, this one. Trust her, and she *will* get you away.'

George was out of the back door, then, like a shot. I followed, not waiting to watch our mother's parting embrace to Alice and Rajev, and picked up a torch from the kitchen as I went. From the kitchen door, I saw George station himself at the foot of the garden, and then begin scanning our street for any possible sign of Mr Harlaw. I waited till he gave me his 'all clear' signal and then led Alice and Rajev quickly down to the low fence between the foot of the garden and the disused limestone quarry sloping away from the fence. At the far side of the quarry, I pushed aside a thick growth of ivy, and beckoned Alice and Rajev into the hole it had concealed.

The hole wasn't part of the quarry, I explained to them. It was a section of a tunnel, accidentally broken into ages ago, by the quarry workers; and the tunnel led to Redhouse Castle. Alice asked in surprise:

'How did you discover it?'

Once a secret was out, I thought, it was out. But I was still resenting the fact that I'd had to give it away, still bitterly regretting that an end was now in sight for all the fantasy-games I'd worked out so beautifully alone there; and so I was curt when I told her:

'Read about it in a book from the library – *Ancient Scottish Castles*. It used to be an escape route to the sea when the castle was under siege. Then one day when I was picking wild strawberries in the quarry, I found it.'

I flicked on my torch and started leading them along the tunnel. We had to bend half-double; but that didn't matter, because there was no need to hurry. The road between the village and Redhouse Castle was a slow and winding one, and the tunnel cut straight across country underneath this route, so that we were sure to be in plenty of time to catch the bus at the Redhouse Castle stop.

The cellar at the end of the tunnel was in ruins. We squeezed through the small gap that the fallen masonry had left at the tunnel's end, and clambered to the ground floor of the castle. I flicked my torch towards the bus-stop sign beyond a gap in the outer wall, and led the way towards it. Alice checked her watch in the torchlight and said:

'Ten minutes, Rajev, and we'll be safely on that bus.'

'And in ten hours,' Rajev answered, ' we can be out of the country, on our way to another university, and beyond your father's reach for ever.'

'Yes, for ever,' Alice agreed, and I noticed that she didn't seem at all sad now, over this prospect. She was happy as Larry, in fact, with so much of smiling and whispering going on between her and Rajev that both of them seemed to have altogether forgotten I was there. *And* they never noticed the rain that came suddenly belting down so hard that even the ten minutes' wait for the bus was long enough to soak us.

'Many waters cannot quench love,' I muttered, 'neither can floods drown it.'

Rajev managed to look away from Alice for long enough to ask me vaguely: 'What was that you said?'

The glare from the bus headlights caught us. 'I was quoting,' I told him. 'Just a couple of lines from *The Song of Solomon.*'

Rajev looked puzzled, but Alice understood, and

quickly explained to him, 'It's a poem, Rajev – from the
Bible; one that celebrates the triumph of love.'

Rajev smiled then; and in the beam of the headlights
closing in on us, his eyes were brown-gold and brilliant
with delight. The bus squelched to a halt. Alice seized
Rajev's hand, and the two of them climbed aboard calling
back at me:

'Good-bye, good-bye, And thank you, thank you *very*
much.'

The driver of the bus revved its engine, and I jumped
back from the spray of mud thrown up by its churning
wheels. It began to draw away from the road verge. I
remembered Alice and Rajev sitting close together,
isolated in the very perfection of their togetherness, and
the thought of them still together and riding off aboard
that bus swept me suddenly into a wild and strange kind of
ecstasy that would not let me just stand there. I began to
dance and caper in the roadway; and when heads turned to
let curious passengers peer at me through the blur of rain
on the rear window of the bus, I waved my torch to them
and exultantly yelled:

'The triumph of love! The triumph of love! Did you
hear that? The triumph of love!'

The stares remained curious, uncomprehending. The
bus gathered speed; yet still I danced and waved and
shouted. The rear lights of the bus dwindled to red sparks
in the darkness, then disappeared completely; and *still* I
went on dancing and waving. And still, as mud flew up
under my feet and the circling light of my torch cut golden
across the rain-soaked darkness, I sang out the ecstasy I felt
for Alice and Rajev, and for the triumph of love.

I was quite giddy by the time I stopped at last. But I
didn't really mind about that. I didn't care in the least,
either, whether or not those people staring at me from the

bus had thought I was acting like some crazy person. It was only right, after all, that *someone* should have celebrated the triumph of love. I was sure of that. What was more, I had the feeling that it had been a kind of privilege for me to have been that someone.

And so I turned away from the bus-stop that night, not even caring that the secret of the tunnel was now no longer mine, because all those fantasies I'd worked out there – they were, after all, only the kind of pretend games I'd been playing all my life till then. But tonight had been real, and my part in it had been real. The sense of privilege that had given me was real too, very definitely so – as if, in fact, I'd been given some sort of award to show I'd crossed over from my pretend world to the one that belonged to people like Alice and Rajev.

I felt proud of that – proud of being different now from the way I had been. And happy about it too – so happy that I sang to myself all the way home through the tunnel, and even took George down there afterwards so that he could inherit the games from me.

MOLLIE HUNTER

Summer of Ladybirds

'Paul! Where are you going?'
'Out! Anywhere. Out.'

The long hot summer dragged on endlessly. The heat became intolerable. It was too much effort to walk about. People stayed indoors, drawing their curtains against the sunlight. Even the nights were pitilessly hot. It was impossible to sleep. In the daytime fractious children squabbled and cried, and parents scolded them, too irritable to give them any comfort.

Inland the parched earth cracked and shrank. Grass died. The soil lay like grey dust, and forests were ravaged by fire. Scorched hillsides smoked.

And on the coast a small strange invasion was preparing. It was a plague of ladybirds. They swarmed across the barren earth to the hot sands, and bred there in their millions, taking possession of the beaches like summer tourists. Children came outdoors to capture them in jam jars, and squelched them underfoot. They crawled in sluggish bundles on stones, on kerbs, on railings, clinging obsequiously to clothes and hair, clinging to shrinking skin. They blundered in waspish, unfamiliar flight, or lay like red gleaming pools on the roadside, shifting lazily. Motorists drove blind in blood-red cars. And on the sands they lay drowned, cast backwards and forwards like bright beads by the tides.

The summer had gone wrong. The heat was hideous.

Late one August evening, when a copper sun was low over the estuary, Paul came down to the sands. Some council workers were shovelling up ladybirds into huge bins on the prom. Paul leaned against the railings, watching them, flicking his hand across his face from time to time.

'Some holiday!' he thought. 'Some rotten holiday!' He had spent the last few weeks cooped up in the holiday flat with his parents until a small knot of fury built up inside him. He felt as if he hated them; everything they did irritated him, yet there was no escape – too hot to walk across the sandstone hills, or to lie in the fields, or to bathe in the sea. The heat had exhausted his mother. She lay on the couch like some lumpish Eastern princess, fanning herself with last night's newspaper, puffing out her lips as if breathing was too much effort. Paul had tried to be nice to her – this evening he had made the meal, but she had chewed it as though she expected to find a ladybird in every mouthful, and pulled out pieces between her teeth to line the plate with, like a reproach.

'Can't eat, love,' she sighed. 'Just can't eat. Take it away.'

His father sat inside his pipe smoke, cracking his fingers and listening to the radio; all day long, news and interviews and current affairs, rapid insistent voices, on and on and on . . . and the stem of his pipe stabbing out of his smoke cloud – 'What d'you think of that, Paul? Eh? What d'you think of that?'

'I'm going!' Paul had shouted. 'Out!'

As soon as he got outside he felt better, though the heat of the evening was still oppressive. His head throbbed. He felt as if he wanted to pick up a stone and smash it through the window of the holiday flat, knock his father's pipe for six and send the radio chattering and whistling into pieces across the floor.

He started to run, fiercely brushing ladybirds off his hair, shaking them from his hand. They landed heavily from a drunken flight and occasionally they nipped, sharply and tinily. Paul tried to avoid the red clusters on the pavement as he ran, but once he was on the prom he found it was impossible to go down the steps on to the beach without treading on them. He closed his eyes, and felt the step slithering under his foot.

He walked quickly along the shoreline away from the houses and towards Red Rocks. He always loved it there. It was a tiny bay curving into tall slabs of red sandstone. When he came here as a little boy he used to leap off the rocks into the soft sand. It was always good to watch the sunset there, slipping down between Hilbre Island and the long arm of the Welsh hills. He walked there now out of habit, not really aware of where he was walking, only of the anger and frustration that was driving him away from the house.

'That's the last time I go away with them,' he said to himself. 'It's worse than being at home with them. No bike. No telly. No Griffo. Holiday! I'd rather be at school! I'd rather do maths all summer!'

He pulled himself up on to the rocks, stamping on the hard black bubbles of bladderwrack, trying to crack them. The stomp of his foot thudded as though the ground was hollow, but there was another, brisker, sound; a snap with a kind of rhythm to it. He stopped and listened, trying to identify it. He crept forward and peered over the edge of the rock. Crouching about three metres below him, and bending forward away from him, was a small girl. Her elbows jerked with rapid movement. He moved crabwise and soundless along the rock edge, trying to fathom what she was doing. A small stone crumbled away from his foot and bounced down near to her, but she didn't look up. In front of her she had a small pile of sticks, branches, which she was breaking up into smaller pieces, lying them side by side like logs ready to be rolled down to a river. When she had a handful ready she swung round and laid them in a crisscross pattern over a hole in the rock, balancing them with care so they didn't roll forward and spoil the pattern. She turned again to the pile of sticks and began to break up another set, laying them on to the crisscross pile.

Paul jumped down from his ledge, spraying up sand with his hands and feet as he landed on all fours next to her. The girl looked up at him for a moment, frowning. She wasn't a child. She had a small, round, squashed face, with close-set eyes. Her fine brown hair was cut like a child's, fringed and short. Her bare arms and legs were plump, and her fingers short and stubby. She was thickly freckled, and her lips were moist with saliva dribble.

'Hello,' Paul said. 'What are you doing?'

She stared at him warily, laying her hands over the stick pile. She reminded him of a cat caught with a bird. He walked away from her and she bent down again immediately to her twig-snapping. He sat in a curve of the rock where the sand was cool. He was watching the swifts darting, but he could see her.

After a time she stood up and shook bits of clinging twig from her skirt. She rubbed her hands together, satisfied with her work. Then she fumbled in her pockets and brought out a box of matches, which she sniffed and shook close to her ear. She struck a match and held it up to

watch the blue flame spurt and dwindle. She struck again
and bent down to drop the match into the middle of the
little crisscross pyre she had built. There was a slow spiral
of grey smoke, then the flame flared like a tongue, separate
from the pile. The girl laughed and knelt down, her hands
over it, her face close to it. She could feel the touch of the
heat on her cheeks. She laughed, low and humming, not at
all like a child's laugh. Paul watched her, curious.

With a sudden swift movement she reached behind her
and dragged a red plastic bucket towards the fire, and
tipped it with two hands. The flame hissed and sank. The
red stream from the bucket became separate, like drops of
blood.

Paul came slowly over to her, disbelieving.

'You're burning ladybirds!'

She bent down again and fed her fire from the waiting
pile of twigs, and set to breaking up another pile. Her
small arms worked rapidly and deftly, snapping the dry
twigs to identical lengths, laying them together neatly,
and her eyes never left the low crackling fire. She fed it
again and then ran across the sands to the slipway. Paul
watched her scooping up ladybirds in handfuls and ladling
them into her child's bucket. He crouched down and put
twigs on the fire for her, to bring the blaze back up, while
she watched him. Then she emptied the bucket gradually,
tipping it in small jerks, so its live contents slithered like
water to the fire, spat and sizzled.

Paul laughed with her. She rocked herself down on to
her knees. The ladybirds glistened on the stone like red
berries bursting. The smoke curled softly, shrouding
them.

'What d'you do that for?' asked Paul. 'It's cruel, that.'

The girl didn't seem to notice him. She broke her sticks
slowly, captured by the fire.

'I'll fetch wood for you,' Paul offered. 'But I'll not burn ladybirds.'

He wandered up to the low gorse hedge that separated the bay from the camp site. There was one caravan left in the field, and as he watched a woman came out of it, stooped under a line of limp washing that was tethered to a hawthorn, and crossed the field to the lane that led to the village. She left the door of the caravan wide open.

Paul gathered up some dead twigs and took them back to the fire. The girl ran to him with the bucket brimfull again.

'You need a bigger one,' Paul told her. 'A kitchen bucket. We've got one.'

She didn't answer. She tipped her bucket slowly, swirling it now to make the dull red stream spiral round and round into the snuffling fire.

'I'll have to go. Shall I fetch you one tomorrow?'

But she was watching her flames, bent forward, eager, with her hair swung forward across her eyes. He shrugged and walked away from her, turning back to watch her in the dimming light. The sun had dipped but the sky was vivid, rich blue streaked with red, with black swifts dark and screaming against it. The girl's skin, her hair and arms, gleamed as she bent and swayed, and he heard the crack like pistol shots of sharp twigs snapping as he walked out over the sands to his village.

After Paul had gone the girl, Ruth, sat for a while by her small fire while the sky grew dark and the evening tide spread out towards the bay. She waited till the cream of foam crept into the stones, making the ashes hiss, and then she drew away. The tide would come no further now. She found her pumps and picked her way over the rocks and into the caravan field where she and her mother lived. Her mother had just come in.

'I thought you'd be in bed, Ruth. Where've you been till this time?'

'On beach.'

'On the beach!' her mother repeated, disgusted. 'Look at you! Look at the state of you! Sandy knees! You're more like six than sixteen.'

Ruth helped herself to some bread and jam and swung herself up on to her bunk. She kicked her pumps off and sand trickled out of them. Her toes gleamed with the yellow crystals.

'Look at you! Pumps full of sand! At your age!'

Ruth sucked an ooze of jam from a split in her bread. 'I met a boy, Mum.'

Her mother looked at her sharply. 'I don't want you messing round with boys. You're too stupid.'

'I didn't talk to him.'

'I should think not.'

'He talked to me though.'

Her mother sighed. 'Ignore him, Ruth. You're not the type to go with boys.' She started to undress herself, her shadow on the caravan ceiling lumpy and squat in the dull light of the gaz lamp. 'Anyway, boys and men, they're all the same. Leave them alone, or make use of them.'

Ruth lay back on her bunk and smiled. When the camp site had been full she used to watch the boys and girls of her own age. She used to love to see them going around together. She'd see the girls in the washrooms fluffing out their hair and giggling about the boys they'd met. She'd see the boys waiting outside for them, showing off for them as soon as they came out. Where the friendships were special she'd see the hands linking or the boy slipping his arm round his girl's shoulder, and kissing her where her hair touched her cheek. And then Ruth used to slip into the washrooms when they were empty and smile at her reflection, sweep back her thin hair and let it swing forward again to kiss her cheeks.

'We're going to have to move on in a few days, Ruth. I've had enough.'

Ruth rolled herself away from her mother's shadow. She had been expecting this. 'Don't go, Mum. We like this place best.'

'Don't be silly. How can we stay here? Empty camp site. Everyone's gone!'

'They might come back.'

'There's been no takings at all this week. Who's going to pay our wages when there's been no takings? We can't live off sea air.'

'Please, Mum. Don't move again.'

Her mother sighed. She stooped down into her bunk and turned off the gaz lamp. It was too hot to lie under the clothes.

'Don't you forget to wash yourself,' she told Ruth.

Ruth didn't answer. Now that she was in darkness she rolled herself right over so that her knees tucked up almost under her chin. She bit hard against the crooked knuckles of her fingers, her eyes pressed tight shut. Outside the caravan she could hear the light rustle of grasses as the night creatures moved about. She could hear the sea washing against the rocks, like the cool swish of silk. Her mother's breathing deepened and steadied.

Please stay please stay please stay.

Ruth and her mother had spent the last six years running away and hiding. Now night had come again Ruth clearly remembered, as if it was all happening again, the night sounds of the house she had lived in as a little girl: doors banging, her mother and father shouting to each other in tired, heavy voices, lights on, lights off, more shouting,

banging, lights, into the night, into daylight. She had lain in
bed then as tonight curled up away from it all, and
frightened. She remembered vividly and with a start of terror
how on a particular night her mother had run into her room
and lifted her out of her bed as though she'd been a baby and
had carried her downstairs and out into the rain to a waiting
taxi; how her father had come running out after them, his face
bending towards her on the other side of the window, how
the picture of him had blurred yellow as the taxi moved away.
She remembered his voice over the engine sound: Please stay.

The mother and girl had trailed from town to town finding
lodgings where her mother could pick up jobs. Wherever they
went it meant a change of school for Ruth; the new horrors of
children shying away from her strangeness, or taunting her
with it.

Twice, in the first two years, her father had found them.
Ruth could remember running in from school to see him
standing there, unexpected, in the kitchen or the hall, her
forbidden and undisguised surge of pleasure at seeing him
evaporating as her mother came between them.

'Come home!' her father had begged.

'Home!' her mother had hissed. 'This is my home. Home is
where I live.'

After he had been they would always move again.

Then, last summer, they had fetched up here. Ruth's
mother had seen the advertisement for a campsite caretaker,
and because the day had been a fine one and they had both felt
like a trip to the seaside, they had come to enquire about it. It
was early summer, and the campsite was full. The hedgerows
that bordered the fields were tangled with forget-me-nots and
sea-pinks and poppies. Far out in the estuary yachts bobbed
like butterflies in a field. 'Let's stay!' Ruth begged. Her mother
smiled down at her. 'We'll try it,' she promised.

Ruth loved it at Red Rocks. She used to watch the new

families as they arrived and make up names for them to
share with her mother: 'Famous Five Go Camping' or
'The Happy Family' or 'The Birdwatchers'. The little
children shyly let her into their games. The older ones
always ignored her, but she watched them lovingly. She
saw romances flare and fade, and she involved herself
deeply in all their precarious emotions.

Her mother was happy there, too. She enjoyed
gossiping with the adults as they came to book themselves
in or to buy odds and ends of food from the little store she
kept in the caravan. During the winter she had found
herself a part-time job at the local cinema. At Easter Ruth
had left school for good. She felt as if the campsite job was
hers now, especially when her mother was out at the
cinema.

'Don't let me down, now,' her mother warned her, the
first time she left her in charge. Ruth tidied up their
caravan. She drew up a new account book, using three
different coloured pens. She made sure the small
washrooms were spotless, always, and when she saw new
arrivals coming she was ready for them and smiling in the
caravan, as though they were friends already, or come to
join her family.

'Talk to the big girls,' her mother said, and Ruth made
an effort to approach them, shy. But she seemed too
young for them. So she chose her friends in secret and
watched them. When she wasn't busy she'd squat by the
tent or the caravan of her chosen friends and watch them
come and go, and when they left the site she would run
after their car, waving and smiling, and they, amused, sad
for her, would wave back.

And now the summer had gone wrong. Over the past
few weeks the visitors had left the field, weary of seeking
shelter in the tiny strip of shadow cast by the tents and the

caravans, defeated by the heat and by the invading crawl of ladybirds in their food and their clothes and their sleeping bags. When the last few were leaving Ruth didn't even wait in the caravan to say good-bye to them. She crouched in the rocks at the bottom of the field, hiding from them.

Ruth slept fitfully the night her mother told her they were leaving, dreaming that the field was crowded with human-sized ladybirds in tents and caravans, every inch of space taken, with more of them peering over the hedges. Rain streamed down, the colour of blood, and every drop bubbled and burst to spawn more ladybirds.

'Ruth!' her mother had to shake her awake the next morning. 'Ruth! Up! I'm going to town. Are you coming?'

'What for?'

'I'm going to find a job, and somewhere to live. We're not staying here, Ruth. I can't stand it.'

'I'm not leaving,' Ruth told her. 'I'm old enough to do as I like now.'

'You!' her mother laughed. 'You're a child!'

'Anyway, he always finds you in towns!' Ruth called after her.

Her mother hurried away from the caravan, her sandals flicking up the dry earth dust. Ruth made herself some breakfast and wandered outside with it. The day was scorching-hot already. She gathered some twigs from the hedgerows and carried them under her arms down to the bay. She lay for a long time flat on her belly on the sand, watching the ladybirds tipping and tumbling into the warm corrugations the tide had left. They fascinated her. She didn't mind them crawling on her flesh. After a time she nursed the low bed of grey charcoal back into life and toiled backwards and forwards across the hot soft sand, carrying her loads, watching out for Paul, and when she saw him coming she smiled to herself and stopped looking.

He came on to the rock and dropped a large kitchen bucket on to the sand beside her. Neither of them spoke. After a while he went over to the hedge to pull branches off, tossed them down on to the sand and jumped down after them. He watched the girl curiously. Her intent round face gave away no age at all. She was like no girl he had ever met. He knew that if he was with his friend Griffo they would laugh at her. He pictured himself sitting on the rocks with Griffo.

'What's fat and red and black all over?'

'That girl covered in ladybirds.'

'Hey,' he said. 'Why are you burning those things?'

She stared at him. 'To get rid of them.'

'But . . .' he swung his arm round in a helpless circle. 'There's millions of them!'

'Then we'll have to hurry,' she said placidly. 'They're spoiling our summer.' She jerked her head towards the campsite. 'They've all gone home now. I hate it when they all go home.'

She bent to her bucket again. She had dragged it across from the slipway, but now it was too heavy for her to lift. She glanced up at him and he laughed.

She stood back, arms akimbo, watching him. Her fat child's feet curled in the sand as she steadied herself.

The red mass in the bucket writhed langorously; reminded him of a fish cast up on land, gasping.

'I can't burn it,' he said.

Don't laugh, Griffo. Could you?

'I can't lift it,' she said.

He lifted the bucket at last, aimed, and closed his eyes. The fire hissed as the bucket grew light in his hands, and he felt his throat clenching and unclenching and his teeth grinding together. Ruth sighed. He handed her the bucket and bundled twigs hastily on to the fire.

They sat down under the rock, away from the sting of the smoke.

'Do you kiss girls?' she asked.

Paul jerked his head away from her, cancelling his smile of astonishment.

Can't answer that one, Griffo.

'Boys never kiss me.' Her voice was dull, and he risked another quick glance at her. She wasn't even looking at him. 'On our site, they're always going round kissing each other. My mum says it's indecent. She says they won't do it to me though, because I'm not like that. She says I'm witless.' She giggled suddenly, shy. 'She says I'm like those ladybirds. I'm harmless enough so long as I don't make a nuisance of myself.'

Paul held his breath.

'What's it like, kissing?' She swung her head round to look at him, lifted her hair away from her eyes, fearless.

He shrugged. 'Dunno,' he said, intent on the warm sand he was riffling through his fingers. 'Dunno.'

Help, Griffo.

She snatched up her bucket and ran off, swinging it like a small child, and dropped to her knees, her hands cupped, her face intent.

'Just half-fill it, then you can manage it on your own,' he called roughly. But if she heard him, she didn't answer.

When Paul reached the holiday flat his father told him that they were leaving the next day.

'Your mother's had enough, Paul,' he said. 'Look at her. It's drained the life out of her.'

'I'd be far better off at home,' she agreed, puffing her

lips out like a fish, Paul thought. 'We'll all be better off at home.'

'Can't we just stay till the end of the week?' Paul asked. 'I mean, the weather might break by then.'

'It might,' his father agreed, surprised. 'Feels as if it's going to bust up soon, if something doesn't happen.'

'And it might not!' his mother sighed. 'What's up with you! He's been loping round the place like a trapped spider all week and now we want to go he wants to stay!'

'Just for a few days,' Paul muttered, embarrassed. He didn't understand himself. When he closed his eyes he saw ladybirds, and he saw the girl, shy, laughing at him.

'Met someone, have you?' His father suggested casually. He stretched out his newspaper like a tent.

'Sort of,' Paul muttered.

The newspaper moved. His mother raised her eyebrows.

'It's not like that.' Paul found himself blushing fiercely. He closed his eyes and the ladybirds came back, and the girl, waiting for his help, toiling backwards and forwards through the day's terrible heat. 'O.K. Let's go home tomorrow. I don't mind.'

'We'll see,' his father said. 'Maybe there's something in the air, Paul. More than we know about.' He lowered his paper and winked at his son. 'Eh?'

Ruth's mother returned to the campsite during the afternoon. She went down to the bay to look for the girl but didn't see her, crouched as she was under the overhang with Paul. She could be anywhere. The woman went back to the caravan and quickly packed up her own things, checked that there was enough food for the girl to last her the rest of the week, and wrote a telephone number in the last page of the account book. Then she went, shuddering

as she stepped over the crawl of red on the steps. She
found a phone box near the station and phoned the same
number. Her husband answered.

'Will you have Ruth back?' she asked.

Her husband was overjoyed. 'Ruthie! Of course I'll have
her back. I want you both back . . .'

'Give her a few days,' his wife interrupted him. 'She'll
phone you.' She put the receiver down quickly, before the
break in her voice gave her away. The best thing, she told
herself as she picked up her bags again.

The best the best the best.

By the time evening came the air was so still and heavy
that Paul felt as if he needed to cut away chunks of it in
order to move about in it. He went outside. The sky was
almost green. Within seconds of leaving the house he was
clammy with sweat. He no longer brushed the crawling
ladybirds away from his skin. His footsteps echoed between the walls of the silent houses with a queer ringing
sharpness. The peculiar bloom in the sky deepened to
bruising. Seagulls flung themselves into its colour,
brilliant white flecks.

He was on the sands when the first crack came. Then the
rains came, huge, slow drops, sliding over him, separate
beads bursting. He held up his arms and his face to it,
drinking it. The sky snapped with electricity.

He thought about the girl, and he began to run, the
damp sand claggy already under the soles of his shoes. His
shirt was soaked; rain streamed through his hair and into
his eyes. He leapt pools as he came to them, hardly
breaking his stride and laughing as he splashed, roaring
back at the rolling thunder; exhilarated by the energy of
the storm and by the gashes of lightning that ripped the
sky.

By the time he reached Red Rocks small rivers were gushing from them. He slithered across the boulders and jumped down to the black and sodden remains of the fire, and there, underneath the overhang of rock where they had talked that afternoon, lay the girl. She was curled up, asleep, with her bundle of twigs beside her.

Rain pittered down from the overhang and washed over her skin. She murmured when he shook her. 'I'm not going away. Leave me alone.'

He stood up, helpless, oblivious of the rain beating down on him.

'Let me take you home,' he said, crouching down to her.

She curled herself up away from him into the rock. Her hands were blistered, her limbs were aching. Her skin was feverish to touch.

'You can't stay here,' Paul urged.

Her mouth was dry. 'Please let me stay.'

He stood up again. He had no idea what to do. He didn't know whether she was ill with the heat or exhaustion or just pretending, playing a child's game with him. The burnt twigs slithered apart. Water from the rocks gushed into the plastic bucket, toppling it.

'You must go home. Please.'

Another brief blast of thunder seemed to kick the very rock they were sheltering under. Its violence was suddenly a terrifying, alien thing. Paul's instincts were to run from it, head down into the weather, feet slapping across the sand, and not to stop until he reached home and his parents. Instead he bent down and lifted Ruth up. Her weight fell against him as he stood up, so that he had to bend backwards slightly, his arms hooked up round her neck and the backs of her knees, his shoulder pressed forward to hold her head up. She was heavier than he'd expected. The muddy sand dragged his feet. He staggered across to the lower rocks with her, remembering the leaning caravan in the field. Perhaps someone there would help. He felt the weight of her like his own body. His feet hardly moved. His neck and his arms ached. She lay with her hair swung back and her face closed. Scared, he bent his head down and felt the warmth of her breath on his cheek. He squelched through the mud near the caravan and eased himself up the wooden steps. The door swung open, blowing an open notebook off the table.

The caravan looked deserted. It was as if no one lived here any more.

Paul tipped Ruth forward on to the narrow bunk bed, and settled the blanket round her. Rain drummed into the silence, spilling from the drowning trees on to the roof, trickling through a small hole on to the caravan floor. Paul smoothed her wet hair from her face, like a father to a child, then, leaning forward, kissed her.

He didn't stop running till he reached home. His parents were standing by the window, watching out for him anxiously. His mother brought him a towel and his dry pyjamas while his father made him a hot drink.

'What a marvellous storm, Paul,' his mother said. 'I feel like running out into it myself.' She hung his wet clothes round the gas fire.

'And it's the end of the ladybirds,' his father said. 'They'll never survive this. They'll all be drowned by now.'

Paul saw the girl with the bucket, trailing across the sand.

'I found a girl,' he said. 'A little girl. She was asleep in the rain at Red Rocks. I took her home.'

'Well, if you like we'll walk out there tomorrow, when the rain stops. Something to do.'

Paul shook his head slowly. He watched the steam rising like smoke from his clothes by the fire. Water dripped from them, and a dead ladybird lay with grains of sand in a tiny pool on the hearth.

'No, Dad,' he said. 'There's no point. She's nothing to do with me.'

BERLIE DOHERTY

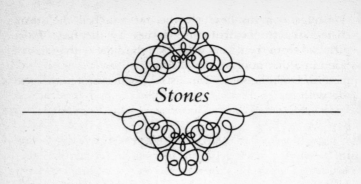

Stones

Jenny picked her way from stone to stone across the wet beach, irritably. This was not her idea of a holiday. Almost everyone else in the Fifth Year was going abroad – Crete, Bulgaria, Benidorm. But *her* parents had to plump for a Scottish island. She had left them in the hotel dining-room, lingering over their breakfast coffee under the sad gaze of stags' heads.

The sides of the stones were covered with a crusty yellow rash of infant barnacles, and they were dotted with winkles which sometimes, for no apparent reason, fell off into the surrounding water. Further down the beach, Jenny crunched across mussel beds, blue-black and softish underfoot, then came to a sand-bank freshly exposed by the falling tide. A few years ago, she thought fretfully, she would have pulled her shoes off and enjoyed the sensation of the firm, wave-ribbed sand under her toes; longer ago still, she would have come running to this untouched freshness with bucket and spade, rejoicing in the chance to dig and build and scrawl great sandy pictures on a brand-new sweep like this. But she was fifteen now.

There was an angry sense of loss mingled with her irritation as she walked along the sea's edge, watching the thin layers of water overtake one another. She could have enjoyed it once. Now it was too late. She was not a little girl any more, to splash in the warm lagoons left by the tide or crouch unselfconsciously over the making of sand pies. Her legs were hidden inside their jeans because she was aware of their shape, worried by the pudginess of her knees, embarrassed when workmen on ladders whistled at her.

She paused and looked round. The beach was empty but for a woman with a couple of toddlers at the far end, where the few small shops backed on to the shingle. Jenny bent down and pulled the laces of her plimsolls undone. There was nobody watching. And anyway, she argued in sudden defiance of her own fears, she was not totally ludicrous. Not like the two old women her mother had laughed at yesterday, grey-haired old birds holding their skirts up while they paddled, shrieking as the water lapped round their varicose ankles.

Jenny curled her toes in the cold sand and watched as the water ran across her feet. She rolled the bottoms of her jeans up, then set off through the shallow water towards the shops' end of the beach. She had said she was going to buy some postcards.

The woman with the toddlers was making a small sandcastle. Jenny went on past her, dragging her feet rhythmically through the shallow waves. She had a strong desire to go on and on wading through this water, and not come back to discuss with her parents whether to go on the putting green again or have a look round the Folk Museum. But her wading was stopped by a rock-built jetty which ran out into the sea in front of her and, reluctantly, she left the water and walked up the beach towards the back of the shops.

Several small boats were pulled up on the shingle,

brown-varnished dinghies, all alike except for the names painted on their transoms. *Maid of the Isles, Mary Ellen, Sea Belle*. A boy of about eighteen, sitting with his back propped comfortably against the wheel of an old-fashioned, red-painted tractor, looked at Jenny as she read the names and said, 'Are you wanting to hire a boat?' His feet, too, were bare, and there were large holes in the knees of his jeans.

'No, thanks,' said Jenny, and went past him from stone to stone until she reached the grass, where she walked round to the front of the craft shop to peruse the rotating stand of postcards. She looked back, suspecting that the boy had turned his head to stare after her, but he had not moved.

'What a lovely idea!' said her mother when Jenny suggested they might hire a boat that afternoon. 'And don't say you're going to be seasick, Maurice, it's as flat as a rice pudding.'

Jenny's father twitched his nose in protest at the analogy, causing his glasses to perform a small hop in front of his vague blue eyes.

'I suppose rice puddings *are* sort of bumpy,' said Jenny, feeling, as she so often did, like an interpreter.

'Oh, for goodness' sake!' Her mother ran her fingers through her wiry dark hair impatiently. 'Why am I surrounded by pedants?'

Maurice tucked in his chin carefully, a substitute for a sigh. 'If you want to go out in a boat, Barbara,' he said, 'we will go out in a boat.'

'We don't need hand-lines, thank you,' Barbara said to the boy with holes in his jeans. 'And neither do we want one of your noisy, smelly little outboards. I shall row.'

'Okay,' said the boy peaceably. 'Walk along the jetty, then, and I'll put your boat in the water.' He climbed into the tractor's metal seat and started its engine, then swung it round to scoop up the *Mary Ellen* on the metal arms of its front-loader. As he started past them with the boat held in the air on his way down the beach, he caught Jenny's eye and gave her a perfectly straight-faced, unsmiling wink.

Barbara had already started along the jetty and did not see the wink but she turned, business-like in her Guernsey sweater and cream linen trousers, in time to notice Jenny's smile. She raised her eyebrows.

Dishonestly, Jenny spread her hands to indicate the sky and the water and a general happiness, and Barbara slipped her arm through hers and said, 'It *is* lovely, isn't it. I knew you'd appreciate it, once you got used to the simplicity.'

'Good going in three days,' said Maurice.

With the boat in the sea, the boy climbed into it from the tractor and threw a rope up to Jenny's father, who missed it. Making no comment, the boy fitted the oars into the rowlocks and brought the boat to the jetty's side in a couple of strokes.

'Maurice, I think you'd better get in first,' said Barbara. 'I'll hold the camera.'

Stoically, Jenny's father permitted himself to be helped into the boat, where he sat down at once.

'You'd better move to the back,' Barbara advised as she stepped down neatly, accepting the boy's hand without looking at him. 'Unless you want to row, of course,' she added.

'Good God, no,' said Maurice, and clutched his way to the rear seat. The boy turned to Jenny, and as she met his gaze she felt charged with an irrational excitement. His eyes were grey under the dark eyebrows, and the hand

which supported her as she stepped down into the boat
was hard-palmed and warm. His faded blue sleeveless
tee shirt had a wonderful quality about it, quite unlike the
bright, crude colours of the shirts on shop shelves. The
boy looked at her for a moment's relaxed appreciation,
and smiled.

Jenny sat down on the wooden seat across the boat's
bow. The hole in the boy's jeans was level with her own
knees as, standing in the boat, he pushed off from the jetty
with an oar which he then presented to Barbara, who had
already taken charge of the other one. Then he swung
himself back on to the tractor as they slid past it.

Barbara turned the boat efficiently and headed out to
sea, so that Jenny was looking past her mother at the
tractor. The boy was backing it out of the water, his head
averted as he looked up the beach.

Jenny stared down through the clear water to the pattern
of sand and stones below. Her mother, rowing, began to
declaim one of her favourite poems: 'Oh, Caledonia, stern
and wild, Meet nurse for a poetic child! Land of brown
heath and shaggy wood, Land of the mountain and the –'

'Must you?' enquired Maurice.

'You have no soul,' said Barbara.

Jenny rested her chin on her crossed arms on the edge of
the boat and went on staring. Stern and wild. She was the
child of a stern and wild mother. Barbara managed to be
both, simultaneously.

'Doesn't this wonderful place *stir* you?' Barbara demanded of her husband, sitting in the middle of the seat at
the back of the boat. 'Don't you feel an ancient splendour
throbbing in your pulses? Or do you think seven pounds
fifty for two hours is too much?'

'I don't mind the money, Barbara,' said Maurice mildly.
'You know I don't.'

Barbara rested on her oars, gazing at the long, humped shape of the island. The sun had broken through the earlier mist and streaked the sea with a clear, azure blue. 'It makes me want to *do* something,' she said passionately. 'Something memorable and magic. Something the blue-rinsed matrons of Beckenham would never comprehend. Jenny knows what I mean, don't you, Jenny?' She glanced over her shoulder.

'Oh, yes,' said Jenny without looking up. There was a lot to be said for a stern and wild mother. If, one day, she herself did something outrageous, at least she knew that Barbara would understand. Jenny gave a little sigh of contentment. Suddenly, the future seemed full of promise.

The tractor chugged down the beach to meet them as Jenny, with much instruction from Barbara, brought the boat in, but she saw with a sudden, sickening sense of disappointment that it was driven by the old man in a navy sweater and wellingtons who ran the boat-hire business. She scrambled up on to the jetty without taking his offered hand. After two hours in the boat, the concrete surface seemed to lurch slightly under her feet, and the palms of her hands tingled from rowing.

'Now,' she heard Barbara say to the old man briskly, 'seven-fifty covers the petrol for an outboard motor, doesn't it, and the use of hand-lines. And we just rowed, so –'

Jenny wandered off along the jetty. Perhaps she would send Laura one of those dreadful postcards with a Scottie dog in the middle of four views, to be waiting when she got back from Majorca. Or perhaps not. It would be so awful if she didn't realise it was a joke. Laura could be –

Rounding the telephone box, she came face to face with the boy. 'You're back, then,' he said.

'Yes,' said Jenny, and gave a breathless laugh at the silly answer. His grey eyes were fringed with dark eyelashes. To her fury, she could feel her face flush.

The boy looked at her consideringly, his head a little on one side. Then he put his hands on her shoulders and kissed her on her parted lips.

Jenny made some kind of inarticulate sound, and the boy smiled and walked casually away to meet the tractor, which was coming up the beach bearing the *Mary Ellen* aloft. Jenny's parents were approaching along the jetty, arguing.

It was not as a conscious excuse that Jenny began to pick up stones in her walks along the beach, although it did help to justify her constant absences when she produced still-damp pebbles from her jeans' pockets on her return to the hotel.

On the first day after the boat-trip, the old man in wellingtons had watched Jenny approach with dour understanding. 'If ye're wanting Robbie,' he had informed her, 'he's away for some paint the morning.'

Quickly denying any such motive, Jenny had stooped to pick up a greenish crystalline stone. Inspecting it closely, she had managed to find some small defence against the old man and the anguish his words had caused her. After that, looking for noteworthy stones had become almost interesting. Jenny had even bought a slim book on geology from the craft shop. During the evenings of old Jimmy Shand tapes in the hotel lounge, she stared half-seeingly at the pictures of quartzite and granite, dazzled by the dark-lashed grey eyes which looked at her from a face she could otherwise only recall as a dark, embracing presence against the brilliant sky.

She had seen the boy once or twice, but it had been a

week of fine weather and the boats were in great demand from the tourists, so that he was kept busy filling outboard motor tanks and driving the tractor. Sometimes a party of boat-hirers would demand that he should come with them, to manage the engine and thread the hooks of their hand-lines with the brown, hairy ragworms which Barbara had shuddered over. Jenny watched, and was in despair. The holiday was almost ended, and the return home loomed ahead like death. And then, the next day, it rained.

'You can't go out in this,' Barbara said to Jenny over breakfast. Outside the window, the grey sky merged horizonless into the grey sea and a gull side-slipped along the driving rain.

'My anorak's fairly waterproof,' Jenny argued.

'But what about your shoes?'

'I won't wear any. I can go along the beach barefoot.'

Jenny's father looked at her over the top of his newspaper and said with irony, 'You seem very keen on these stones.'

Jenny avoided his eye. 'It's so awful being in,' she said evasively. Did he *know*? Surely not. He was much too vague. 'I mean,' she persisted, 'it's lovely and wild out there. And we won't be here much longer.'

'Mad girl,' said her mother fondly. 'Of *course* you must go out. If I had some wellies here I'd come with you. Put your plimsolls on – they'll dry out quite quickly afterwards. We'll give them to nice Mrs McFee to put in her kitchen. I expect she's got a great old range or something.'

'Calor gas,' said Maurice. 'You can see the cylinders out-side the back door.'

'Oh, shut up,' said Barbara.

The tide was high, crashing against the wall between the road and the sea, sending up showers of spray to mingle with the rain. Jenny put her head down and ran, splashing

recklessly through puddles until she came to the widening
strip of grass where, even at high tide, there was some
gravelly sand at the top of the beach. There, she slowed to
a walk, badly overheated in her anorak despite the water
which trickled in salty-tasting rivulets down her face. If he
wasn't there, she thought, she would simply have to kill
some time in that boring craft shop. She had promised to
be back within the hour.

But he was there. Jenny saw him through the open door
of the small wooden shed near the tractor, sitting with the
old man amid a clutter of ropes and paint pots and tins of
bait. Her nerve failed, and she hardly paused before she
walked on past the rusting litter bin with pictures of ice
creams on its tin sides, into the craft shop.

'Not a very nice day,' said the woman who ran the
shop. 'But I think the sky's starting to clear. Can I help
you at all?'

Jenny shook her head, scattering droplets. 'Just
browsing,' she said.

'That's fine,' said the woman.

Jenny stared dispiritedly at the baskets full of espadrilles
and the brown pottery mugs. Anger mingled with her
misery. Why had he kissed her if he never wanted to speak
to her again? And what did she think she was doing,
anyway, running down here day after day for the sake of a
casual wave or a smile? She poked dismally in a cardboard
box full of small polished stones, each one mounted with a
gilt clasp to enable it to be used as a pendant on a chain.
Perhaps she really would have to buy something.

'Plenty of those on the beach,' he said from close behind
her. Jenny gasped, turning to him.

'I'm away out for some fish,' he said. 'Would you like to
come?'

'Oh, yes, please!' said Jenny, and followed him out of

the shop, dazed. Wind-torn clouds raced across the sky, but the rain had almost stopped. As if in a dream, she scrambled into the sideways-leaning boat where it stood on the shingle.

'You be careful now, Robbie,' the old man warned as he helped the boy to push the boat into the waves which were breaking almost at its bow. 'Don't go far. The wind is getting stronger.'

Robbie, knee-deep in the sea, gave him a withering look and said, 'Do you think I'm stupid?' He hauled himself in over the transom and yanked at the outboard's starter-rope.

'I wouldn't be sure!' the old man shouted after them as the engine fired and the boat went bouncing out across the choppy water. The gulls wheeled and screamed. Ancient splendour, Jenny thought, remembering her mother's words. Something memorable and magic. Yes, she was her mother's daughter, a mad girl.

'Come and steer while I put some lines out,' said Robbie after a while. And, as Jenny climbed towards him, 'Do you know how it works?'

'Not really,' Jenny confessed. Would he think she was a terrible wimp? She bit her lip as she listened to the simple explanation, suddenly a little afraid of his strong Scottish voice and his easy balance in the pitching boat. She loved him, but he seemed very foreign.

Robbie looked at her and said, 'What's the matter?'

'Nothing,' said Jenny. Then, because his grey eyes did not leave her face, 'I thought you'd think I was silly.'

'Och, don't worry about that,' said Robbie kindly. 'All the English are silly. I don't mind.'

'My mother's half Scots,' Jenny offered.

'Is she? Well, you're no' so bad, then. What's your name, anyway?'

'Jenny. Jenny Barton.'

'Mine's Robert Crombie. Robbie, they call me.'

'I know,' said Jenny. She desperately wished he would kiss her again, but he just nodded towards the tiller and said, 'You've no need to change course. Just keep going the way we are.' Then he stepped across the middle seat to the front of the boat, where he busied himself with hooks and bait. Jenny stared at the lurching horizon, not wanting to watch what he was doing. A fitful sun was breaking through the ragged clouds but the wind made her eyes run and, ahead of them, she could see that the waves were white-capped.

Robbie unwound the lines from their wooden frames and secured them over the sides of the boat, then came back to sit beside Jenny, with the outboard between them. He put his arm round her, but he seemed to feel no need to say anything. Potential conversations twittered in Jenny's mind but remained unspoken. After a while Robbie got up and tested the lines, feeling each one in turn. Then he began to wind one in.

The fish broke the surface in an impressive white streak, but when it came jack-knifing out of the water on the end of the line, it was surprisingly small. Robbie took the hook from its mouth and tossed the fish into the front of the boat, where it leapt again and again on the wooden boards.

'What sort of fish is it?' asked Jenny.

'It's a wee whiting,' said Robbie, threading another worm on to the hook. When he had paid the line out again, he came back to sit beside Jenny and this time he pulled her towards him and kissed her.

'I thought I'd never see you again,' she said, and found that her voice was husky.

'We were awful busy,' said Robbie. Carefully, he slid the zipper of her anorak down. His fingers were brown-stained from the bait tin, and yet his touch was curiously delicate as he explored the contours of her body through her tee shirt and jeans. 'You're lovely,' he said.

'I've got fat knees,' said Jenny, almost as a way of stopping this investigation. Although she found the touch of his hand exciting, she did not like the objectivity of his exploration. She wanted him to be close up against her, a dark, embracing entity which would shut out the sky and leave no space between them.

Robbie laughed and kissed her again. 'They're great knees,' he said. 'I don't like skinny girls, anyway.'

'I'm glad,' said Jenny, and buried her face in the warm, fishy-smelling opening of his waterproof jacket. Cradled with him in the rhythmically-bouncing boat, she wanted this moment to go on for ever.

For a long time, she was oblivious of everything except Robbie's close presence, kissing and fondling. For the first time since the lost memory of babyhood, she felt perfectly accepted and right.

At last Robbie looked up. The wind had stiffened and the patch of sunlight had disappeared. A heavy bank of black cloud had piled up on the horizon. 'We'll need to get back,' he said, detaching himself from Jenny. 'We shouldn't have come so far. I'd not noticed.' Quickly, he started winding in the nearest line without stopping to check whether it had secured a catch.

'Should I turn the boat round?' asked Jenny.

'Wait until the lines are in or you'll twist them up,' said Robbie. 'Take that one in, can you?'

With the tiller wedged under her elbow, Jenny wound the wet line clumsily round and round its frame. Even Robbie, she noticed, was finding it difficult to keep his footing in the increasingly violent movement of the boat as they seesawed up and down the waves. A very small fish flipped over the edge of the boat on the end of her line, and Robbie quickly detached it and threw it back into the sea. 'Not worth keeping,' he said.

'Throw the other one back as well,' Jenny begged.

Without argument, he grabbed the still-kicking fish from the bottom of the boat and tossed it into the heaving grey water. He pushed the lines into a small locker under the seat then clambered back to Jenny and, with his hand over hers on the tiller, pushed it hard over. 'Hang on,' he said.

As the boat turned and came parallel to the waves, a wall of green-grey water reared on their right, its top breaking and toppling. 'Come *on*,' muttered Robbie to the outboard as the boat shuddered, struggling to climb out of the trough. For a horrifying moment, Jenny was sure the towering wave would engulf them, but somehow the boat ran ahead of it, through the shower of water that poured down on them. The engine raced momentarily as the propeller came clear of the water on the crest of the next wave, then chugged again as they bucketed down into the following trough.

'We'll be all right now,' said Robbie, though the boat was pitching up and down like the most violent of roller-coasters. 'It's only broadside on it's dangerous. You okay?'

'Yes,' said Jenny. Rain was blowing hard in her face, but she was so wet that it didn't matter. 'It's as if nothing's true in the world except this boat,' she said. 'And the sky and the water, and us.'

'It's always like that,' said Robbie.

There were people on the beach. Jenny caught sight of them, a grim group waiting by the jetty as the little boat crept back, tossed like a water beetle on the pounding sea.

'I'll need to keep the motor running until the last minute,' said Robbie. 'Can you jump out with the rope? They'll help you.' He nodded towards the waiting people, most of whom were sheltering under golf umbrellas, though a few men in oilskins were at the sea's edge.

'Okay,' said Jenny. She worked her way forward, half-blinded by rain and spray, and took a firm grip on the end of the rope. Somehow, she felt a great relief that she was not in danger of treading on the wee whiting.

The beach came towards her very fast.

'Now!' shouted Robbie – and she jumped.

'I simply cannot understand you,' said Barbara over lunch. 'Is this to be the pattern of your future taste in boyfriends? A crude young layabout with holes in his jeans?'

Jenny stared at her prawn salad with her fork immobile in her hand, fighting down tears. She had expected the scolding about going out in such a rough sea and worrying everyone, though the reception committee on the beach had blamed Robbie rather than her. But she had counted on her mother to understand. In a desperate appeal, she mumbled wretchedly, 'It was something memorable and magic.'

Barbara's eyebrows shot up. 'Don't you throw my own words back at me, young woman!' she snapped. 'There is a vast difference between romantic imagination and some squalid little outing with a yob!'

'Barbara, I really don't feel that this is the place –' began Maurice. But Jenny, abandoning her untouched prawns, had pushed back her chair. Among curious glances from the other diners, she fled across the Hunting Stewart carpet to the safety of her room.

The remaining day of the holiday was taken up with a

guided nature walk and a spinning demonstration, followed by a deeply ethnic evening of folk song in the Wallace Bar, all closely supervised by Barbara. Jenny realised that her status had been down-graded to that of Child rather than Young Person, but she was so dazed with misery that she hardly cared. She packed her case the next morning mechanically.

Barbara came in and said, 'Are you keeping all your nice stones?'

Evidently, Jenny thought, her lapse from moral health was now considered to be at the convalescent stage. 'Yes,' she said without looking up. They were all she had to take back to that other, empty world.

She stared out of the taxi as they drove past the old tractor and the shed and the boats drawn up on the shingle, but it all looked like a kind of toytown and he was not there.

They were early for the ferry, which had not yet arrived.

'You can leave the cases there,' Barbara said to the taxi driver. 'We can keep an eye on them while we look round this tweed shop.'

'I don't want to go into a tweed shop,' said Jenny as the taxi drove away.

Barbara, already turning over the price ticket on a travelling rug, affected not to hear, but Maurice put his hand on Jenny's arm as he followed his wife into the shop and said, 'Brave words.'

Jenny stared after him in astonishment. She was used to his mild intercessions on her behalf, but she had never expected such an open statement of support. Standing by the suitcases, she pushed her hands into the pockets of her jeans and almost smiled.

A lorry stopped across the road and Robbie got out.

'Thanks,' he said to the driver. 'That's great.' As the
lorry pulled away, he ran across to Jenny, who abandoned
the suitcases and rushed to meet him. 'I went to the hotel
asking for you,' he said, 'and Mrs McFee said you were
away to the ferry.'

Jenny was in his arms. 'I don't want to go,' she said in
his ear. 'I want to stay here, for always and always.'

Robbie smiled at her and said, 'It's awful boring in the
winter. Come on, we can't talk here. Too many people.'
He led her across the car park and down over the red-
brown rocks which reached into the sea. Then he stopped
and turned to her. 'Was your mother furious?' he asked.

'Was she!' said Jenny with feeling. 'But I don't care. It
was worth it.'

Robbie looked oddly embarrassed. 'It was stupid,' he
said. 'It was – a kind of joke, really. I thought you'd be
scared. I shouldn't have thought of you that way. I'm
sorry.'

Jenny stared at the gently-lapping waves which spilled
across the red rock at her feet. Just a joke. The silly tourist
girl gets more than she bargains for. 'I see,' she said in a
strangled voice. Overhead, the gulls were screaming. She
turned away.

'No, you don't see,' said Robbie, catching her by the
arm. 'That's how it started, yes. But for me not to notice
how bad the weather was getting – that wasna any joke.
I'd meant to be back in half an hour, Jenny. Honest.' The
grey eyes stared into hers, dark-lashed and anxious.

Jenny laughed with relief as the nightmare's shadow
moved away. They kissed again, standing close together.
But the time was running out. 'I haven't even got your
address,' she said.

'Just send it to the boat-hire place,' said Robbie. 'It'll
find me.'

'Yes,' said Jenny. After a pause, she added, 'It's such a long time till next summer.'

'It'll pass,' said Robbie. Then he said, 'Could you not come on your own? There's a Youth Hostel.'

Jenny stared at him. It was a revolutionary idea, but she had a whole year to work on it. 'Why not?' she said, and added with an even greater sense of novelty, 'I might talk to my father about it.'

The ferry nosed past the pier's edge, and a plume of black smoke drifted from her funnel as the steering engines came into play, easing her back into the dock. 'I'll have to go,' said Jenny.

Still with his arm round her shoulders, Robbie scuffed with the toe of his dilapidated training shoe among the small stones which lay in a fissure between the rocks. Then he stooped and picked one up. 'I wish I'd something better to give you,' he said. 'But these are nice if you polish them. Like the ones you were looking at in the shop.'

The stone was a translucent white, intricately veined with lines of warm, brownish pink. 'I'll keep it always,' said Jenny, turning it on her palm. 'It's beautiful.' She looked up. 'Thank you.'

They clung together, and kissed for what Jenny knew was the last time. Then, hand in hand, they climbed slowly back across the rocks. As they came to the car park, a bearded man in a van raised a hand to Robbie in greeting, and Robbie shouted, 'Are you away back, Murdo?'

'I am. Come on, then, if you're wanting a lift,' the man said, leaning across to open the passenger door.

Robbie looked at Jenny. 'Do you mind?' he said. 'You don't want me to stand on the pier waving my white hanky?'

Jenny managed to smile. 'No, of course not,' she said, aching for him to stay for a few more precious minutes, and yet relieved that there would be no embarrassing meeting with her parents.

Robbie squeezed her hand. 'Next year,' he said, and gave her the straight-faced wink which had begun it all. Then he ran across to the waiting van.

The ferry's wake spread out across the sea, a widening crumple of the silky, almost colourless surface. Barbara leaned on the rail beside Jenny, watching the pale shape of the island recede. 'So beautiful,' she said. 'Just look at that bank of cloud coming up from the west. And your father's downstairs in the saloon.'

Jenny's fingers closed round the pink-veined stone, warm in her jeans' pocket. She felt very old and experienced. 'Yes,' she said. 'I expect he is.'

ALISON PRINCE

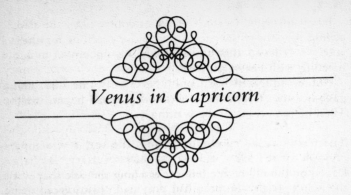

Venus in Capricorn

All tutor period, while Mr Stone went over some option sheets, these four girls were huddled in the corner over that week's *Just Seventeen* 'into' their horoscopes. Just as the bell went I leant across to find out what Taurus had in store.

'Are you a Taurus then, Ducker?' *she* asked in exaggerated surprise. I nodded modestly and snatched the magazine away. Hey, this looked promising.

'Taureans are supposed to be – possessive, jealous – and passionate,' she informed me as I read the good news. "This is your big day: happiness is within your grasp. Don't delay – go for it now. And the boy will be yours."

'Are you possessive and passionate then, Ducker?' she enquired coyly to a chorus of girly giggles. My blood went cold. I didn't want the boy to be mine.

'Does all this work with boys as well as girls, in reverse I mean?' I asked anxiously, but they didn't understand. They were late. They were off. I stood wondering for a moment.

'Ducker!' roared Stoney. 'Don't stand there daydreaming. Get going!'

'Sorry, sir, I do apologise,' I quipped. 'Been reading my

horoscope and it said, "be nice to those in authority". Have a nice day, sir.'

His wrinkled forehead flattened his eyebrows into the fiercest of frowns. 'Horoscopes are for people with empty lives who look forward to horoscopes to promise them a lively future,' he pronounced loftily and pointed at the open door.

Then halfway through Spanish I suddenly thought: why should Lucy Gillimore want to know if I was passionate. Did *I* know if I was passionate?

Why should lovely, long-legged, angel-faced Lucy want to know all this: a girl I had previously considered to be out of my league?

I looked up slowly and gazed across the table, over the rough book, pencil case, upside-down Spanish book, bare fore arm, with some downy hair golden in the sunlight, counted blouse buttons, and there she was gazing right back at me, smack between the eyes. She smiled, held the gaze for a second, blushed and looked down. I blushed and kept staring. At that moment a brass band broke into the Spanish lesson and began to march round the classroom, clashing cymbals, blowing trumpets, waving flags and banging this enormous drum in the shape of Ducker's heart.

I hoped she wasn't too disappointed that I didn't say another word to her in Spanish, or English that lesson, or during break, or during dinner hour. But it was hard playing hard to get. Finally, as I walked past the bus queue after school, I slowed down as I approached her group.

'Don't forget your horoscope, Taurus,' she called to me, cheerfully, yet with a harder tone than earlier. I glanced back nonchalantly, pretending to be ultra-cool. The look was still there, though fainter and fading with every minute.

'Still plenty of time, love,' I crooned. 'The day is still young . . .'

That evening with only six hours of the day left, and only three of them official, I finished my homework early —ninety minutes early; jumped on my bike and pedalled like mad for the tiny village of Ham, where she lived with her mum, elder brothers and forester father in a cottage on the green.

It was a gorgeous evening. The late sun lingered artistically in the sky, deciding whether to tinge the clouds pink, or merely turn the whole world mauve before calling it a day. I raced across the square noticing the four girls sitting on the dossers' bench under the Town Hall clock. Three third years and a second year girl: all made up like paint boxes and eyeing up every motorist, cyclist, pedestrian in trousers. They were welcome. Fine for one night in the disco, in the dark, but nothing more. I, however, was heading for the real thing.

There was a pub dangerously close to the green and I spotted some ex-fifth years swigging lager round this wooden table, and Mervyn Pritchard with one of Lucy's brothers. Don't tell me I'd been too clever and she was now inside playing pin-ball with the lads!

But no: wrong again. As I free-wheeled past the tall grass of the common, I saw this goat tethered to a stake, looking very smug as goats do, and listening to this girl who was lying on her stomach reading to it.

I slowed down gently, letting the brass band march on past, up the hill to the Deer Park. Leaving the bike lying at the edge of the green, I tiptoed over. She was really delicious. God knows what I'd done to deserve this, but I wasn't complaining, yet. Even when she lay on her stomach she had a fantastic figure!

'Once upon a time,' I began once I was within earshot. 'There were three little billy-goats Gruff . . .'

'And a nasty little troll called Ducker,' she continued without looking round.

'Hey, not so much of the little,' I rebuked her riskily and dived down beside her, landing painfully on my elbows. 'Anyway, how did you know it was me?'

'I recognized your sarcasm,' she replied, still not looking, and turned a page. I glanced at the cover and winced. 'Anyway, how did you recognize me?'

I gazed longingly at her back. 'I recognised your b-billy goat. I mean there's only one girl round here with a goat as good-looking as that. And no wonder he looks bored if you read him that rubbish . . .'

'Don't be horrible,' she scolded playfully. 'Jessica loves "Mills and Boon".'

First I was a nasty little troll, then sarcastic, now I was horrible. Don't tell me I'd got it wrong. Serves me right for all that ultra-cool crap!

'Fancy coming to the disco?' was to be my punch line, but all of a sudden I'd lost the nerve to say it. She hadn't even looked at me yet. 'L-lovely evening, eh?' I stammered unmanfully. She sighed, ''Tis indeed.' A pause. 'I . . . er . . . bet the sunset looks nice from the top of the Deer Park . . .'

The book closed slowly, page 124 pressing gently against page 125. She turned and smiled. 'What a lovely idea – you have got a soul after all.'

I thought of joking: no, sorry, left my soul at home etc. – but realised that was pushing what little luck I had left. She sat up on her heels, curly brown hair tumbling over her shoulders, thighs as big as boat hulls in her tight, stone-washed denims. Mine all mine, maybe. She gazed down at me meaningfully.

'Well, come on then – shall we do it, or what?'

Again a joke came to mind, but instead I leapt to my feet, helped her gallantly to hers, but feeling those strong fingers crush mine in their grip realised she didn't need it. 'Mills and Boon' slid into her back pocket. Best place for it. But I couldn't resist it.

I removed the book as clumsily as possible and flicked through the soppy pages. She said, 'See you later, Jesse,' and we walked over the common to the park.

'It's a lovely book,' she sighed as we crossed the road, after a Cortina full of yobbos had roared past, windows full of wolf-whistles and rude gestures. Kids' stuff!

'It's about this young woman who's a brilliant show-jumper and she's got this tumour and thinks she's going to die and then she falls in love with this surgeon who's married but reckons he can cure her with an operation.'

As we strode towards the stile at the edge of the park, I felt like throwing up. 'Oh yeah, that one, I remember,' I teased. 'I read that one. She dies, and her dad's so angry he murders the surgeon with a chain-saw, but the surgeon's wife gets him one night with a meat-cleaver but the other wife runs her down with a combine-harvester. Yeah, really moving . . .'

'Don't be horrible,' she wailed, waiting at the stile. She was certainly fast. This wasn't a stroll it was the 200 metres sprint. 'Anyway, I've read it twice already – it's a beautiful ending. I cried for hours afterwards.'

She cried for hours after reading it for a second time. And was reading it again? I ran my finger over the rough wood of the stile.

'What birth sign are you then?' I asked suddenly. Gemini. 'Now they're supposed to be flirty and two-faced.'

Me and my big mouth. A splinter jabbed into my

finger. 'Ouch!' She folded her arms. 'Stop being horrible all the time – you're supposed to he nice,' she said and took my painful index finger gently.

'Oh, who says?' I asked as she squeezed the pink flesh. I muffled a scream.

'Ruthie,' she answered and her long finger nails pincered the instrument of torture clean out.

'Oh Roo–ooh–Ruthie?' I gasped. 'I haven't been nice to her for ages. She's just angry 'cos I chucked her,' I informed her as she sucked my swollen fingertip. Were splinters poisonous?

'Well, she's got you properly sussed,' she continued, giving me my finger back. 'She said you were nice, but . . .' She paused for torment. 'Well . . .'

'Well? Yeah, I'm very well now, thanks for the splinter job,' I gabbled nervously, afraid of this new truth that was looming large.

'Immature, she said,' Lucy gave me a strange knowing look as she said it.

'Me immature?' I squawked in outrage. 'I am fourteen. That means I can be a bit of both – man and boy, surely. Anyway, Ruthie's only jealous. Just 'cos she's ninety-two.' I was really angry with that know-all vicar's daughter.

'She'll die an old maid, like in real books.' And I vaulted, yes vaulted, confidently over the stile.

'She won't die an old maid,' Lucy said leaning against the lethal wood. 'She'll marry you!'

'Never!' I shouted as she giggled. 'Her marry me? Don't be horrible. You're supposed to be nice . . .'

'Oh? Who says,' she asked eagerly. I didn't like the eagerness.

'Thornie!'

'Mister Thorne, our Headmaster?' she laughed. 'I've never been out with Thornie! You're thinking of Stoney.'

'You've been out with Stoney? He'll get the sack!' I

assumed she was joking, but these days you could never be too sure.

She climbed on to the stile and paused, obviously expecting her gallant escort to help her down, even if she was twice as fit as I was. But it gave me a chance to get my hands on her, so I grabbed her hips, lifted, felt this unexpected weight and as her hands grabbed my shoulders to steady herself we fell back into the deep grass.

'Wow!' I groaned ecstatically. 'Isn't it time you went on a diet?'

'I shall,' she whispered, her breath brushing my hot cheek. 'When you start building up some muscles . . .'

'Yeah, but being a weed has its advantages,' I croaked. 'I mean . . . look at me now . . .'

I gazed past her cheek for a moment, past the coral whorl of her ear, the thick brown curls and up at the sky. A jet roared softly but invisibly overhead; a seagull floated on the white arc of its wings miming to the noise. Soon the jet's roar was replaced with a rush and thunder of blood in my ears and pounding of heartbeats. She blocked out the sky. I had a soul after all. First my finger tip and now my mouth!

Ten minutes later, or maybe more – why not boast – she got off my prostrate body, freed herself from my greedy grope and stood up like a giant.

'Oh well, now that's over with, we might as well go back,' she announced drily. 'You've got what you wanted.'

'What?' I gasped and got up beside her. 'We've come to watch the sunset – remember? Haven't you got a soul?'

And with that I hauled her, panting, up the hill. There, at the summit, we sat and watched the red orb sliding into the pink flank of the Forest of Dean. Our perfect peace was spoiled slightly by this old man standing halfway up the hill, posing with his camera. He had a telephoto lens. He ignored us but stood fiddling with his equipment.

Suddenly I felt this really warm glow and the moment froze; the old man became a tree. She and I became statues lying there head-to-head, arm in arm, dreaming of eternal love. And the sun was a bullet hole in the sky. I'd never felt quite like this before. Red-rose petals scattered over the steel-blue Severn. Then the river turned mauve and faded greyly into the rest of the grey skyline. Click!

'If I was a poet,' I said, glowering at the photographer. 'I'd be really inspired right now.' The truth was I felt slightly scared.

'Oh,' she said encouragingly, and hugged my arm.

'The sky is blue, the Severn a dirty brown,
The countryside's dead boring, I wish I was back in town . . .'

'No you don't,' she insisted. I surrendered. No, I didn't.

So hand in hand we strolled back down the hill to the stile. A magpie chattered overhead, eager to spread the gossip. I looked round hastily for the other one.

'Why do girls mature quicker than boys?' she asked strangely, swinging my arm.

'God knows,' I grunted, unsure of the question's purpose, and left it at that.

Unfortunately, we were spotted on the way back down by Dolly Skinner who lives in the gate house of the Deer Park with her grandparents. She had told the whole world by the time I strolled into room two next morning.

'Hi, Lucy!' Davy Cole shouted at me, seeing me go red as a tomato. Meanwhile the lads were teasing my beloved.

'Who was that you were with in the Deer Park then, Mrs Ducker?'

'Oh dear,' I sighed wearily to myself. 'Boys can be so immature sometimes.' Though I could see what all the

excitement was about. However, I sat down in the corner
of the room, as far away from my 'beloved' as possible. At
least, that way it saved us both embarrassment. The others
were only jealous anyway. Ruthie wouldn't even look at
me.

Lucy didn't seem to mind and pretended to ignore me
during lessons. However, come break and lunchtime and
we were down the bottom of the field, reading 'Mills and
Boon', dramatising the good bits and shooing away
curious, corruptible first year tots.

She invited me to a disco, but that had more than one
catch to it, I found out. Saturday afternoon I was in her
bedroom while she played me this tape and demonstrated
the ideas she had for a dance routine. I sat on the bed and
gaped at her while she gyrated to 'Thriller'. Dance? It was
more like modern ballet, or a piece of choreography from
'Fame'. I certainly wouldn't 'live forever' dancing like
that. I'd be lucky if I got halfway through.

'Oh come on, Ducker,' she exhorted, sweat, I mean
perspiration, beading her beautiful forehead; hands on
hips. 'All you have to do is copy me – only reverse, like a
mirror.'

I shrugged, watched her again and tried it. By the fifth
time of rehearsing it was half-past four and I was really
getting ready to bite Michael Jackson in his neck. She had a
poster of him on the ceiling. We got tangled up, out of
step, hotter and more irritated with each other. In the end
she pushed me back on to the duvet in disgust.

I lay back, panting heavily and stared up at young
Michael. Why him, I wondered.

'Well for one thing he's an ace dancer,' she explained,
rewinding the tape with a high-pitched whine of high-
tech. 'And for another, he loves animals. So he and I do
have a lot in common.'

'I s'pose he's got a flipping goat as well,' I suggested sourly; but fearing I was jealous of her two-dimensional dream lover, she dived on to the bed and we passed a few sloppy, slurpy, slobbery, heavenly, eternal seconds, minutes, days, nights, years, aeons. It may not have been Paradise but it was as good as the garden next door.

'Oh well,' she sighed rolling off me. 'You might as well go now. You've got what you came for, haven't you?'

'No,' I retorted wondering why she kept up this kind of question. 'I haven't got all the moves right yet. The footwork, I mean.'

This worked and she returned to me. We did a bit of exploring. She unbuttoned my shirt, gasped in amazement at my stunning, juvenile torso and said: 'When are you going to grow hairs on your chest?'

Already after a few days I was used to this kind of daft question. I fiddled with my digital watch. 'Now let me see . . . ah yes, in two years time, on Friday the tenth of August at midnight I shall start to sprout thick, curly black hairs all over my body – then I'll do a Michael Jackson, break into your bedroom and bite you in the bum, er neck. How about that?'

'Two years?' she considered dubiously. 'I hope I can wait that long.'

'It must be a full moon,' I added hastily. Her hand was still inside my shirt, as if she was searching for something precious that I'd stolen and concealed upon my person. Still, it was better than dancing, I suppose.

'Ducker? Why do boys have nipples?'

My God, start the music! Get dancing again! Heaven knows what she'd ask next. But then, in that uneasy silence which followed this incredible question, I wondered. Why the hell do boys have nipples?

'Well, Luce, you see it's like this,' I began, trying not to laugh as her fingers tickled my armpit. 'Some parents can't always make their minds up which they want: boy or girl. See?'

'Oh,' she replied openly as if satisfied. She was in a really strange, deep mood, not exactly bored, but in a sort of trance of emptiness. That's what comes of reading horoscopes. All these stupid questions kept floating into her head, like bubbles.

'But why do some boys mature quicker than others then?' she piped again, her eyes wide, following this question as it floated away in its bubble. 'I mean, look at Murph: he's growing a moustache already!'

I felt a twinge of panic. Perhaps she was bored and it was Murph she really fancied now. 'Yeah, and he's got a beard growing inside his head!' I snapped back. All this talk of maturity and hair was giving me an inferiority complex.

'Look, Lucy my little love, the answer's dead easy,' I explained maturely, being her intellectual superior at least. 'We all have to be different, right. Otherwise life would be dead boring, see? I mean, even I'd be boring if I was like everybody else!'

'Oh, Ducker,' she moaned sitting up on one elbow and looking intently at my navel. 'You'd never be boring. They'd have to bury you first, but it's just that . . .'

She took my favourite index finger; the one that had suffered the agony and the ecstacy of that splinter. 'It's just that sometimes I don't feel like a girl. I feel, sort of older. More like a woman. D'you know what I mean . . .?'

Well, if I didn't I kept it a big secret. I was way out of my depth, but nodded wisely for appearances' sake. 'And I feel I want to be loved like a woman . . .'

This was a cue for a joke, or something else. Being a coward in all things physical, I tried a joke. 'So you *have* been out with Stoney?'

She sighed emptily, pulled a face and began to button up my shirt nodding as she spoke. 'That's right, baby Ducker. Now you mind you don't catch a nasty cold on your little chest with no hairs on or anything . . .'

Having rested sufficiently we then rehearsed our routine a couple of times more until, though I say it myself, we did manage to look quite sensational!

The disco was that night at the 'Golden Mills' motel. Lucy and I won the competition by miles: a cassette each. Everybody was dead jealous, of course, but then, who wouldn't be? Nobody congratulated me or anything, though Lucy had more than her share of admirers.

When I came back from the bog she was up against the wall being ogled and chatted up by a couple of the older lads. As I got close I recognised her brother; but he was out of bounds so that was all right – and Merv' Pritchard. Now they were neighbours almost: his farm being the other side of the common.

'How's it going, Merv'?' I chirped, squeezing through to get at the side of my treasure, and ready to fend off the pirates, politely.

He talked to me, but kept looking at her. We used to get on quite well while he was 'inside'. In fact, I quite liked him. Everybody did, worse luck. His father had died recently too, very suddenly, so I felt sorry for him too. I wasn't the only one.

'I never knew you were such a lovely mover, Ducker,' he congratulated me smoothly, smiling at her. 'Still, I bet Lucy could make a lovely mover out of anybody . . .'

As the whole world laughed, a red-hot needle began to skewer me in the guts. 'Yeah,' I joked back, 'even Stoney!'

She let out a shrieking laugh at our 'private joke' and reclaimed me with an arm round my neck. Safe again, for the time being.

We left early though. She phoned her dad who was going to fetch us in his Landrover. We waited in the car park as the occasional car roared past up the A38.

'He's nice, isn't he, Merv'?' she asked, as if checking her own judgement. I grunted. 'He's a bit like you: always the joker! . . . It was tragic about his old man, wasn't it . . .?'

It was, but this red-hot poker twisted and hissed in my gut. 'If you say so . . .' I replied and she did not like it. There was no more small talk after that. Her dad picked us up; the engine roared through the night; the cones of light from the Landrover's headlamps projected a Witches' Sabbath of shadows off the hedgerows as he sped round the country lanes; her dad shouted routine questions; we shouted routine answers back, and she pecked my cheek before I climbed out.

For the next few days Lucy acted very strangely. I thought it might have been because she was bored with me and yearned for Merv', or yearned for me and was annoyed at my jealousy. But no, it was neither of these: she was broody. Not Lucy – Jessica, the goat. Still, what can you expect if you read it 'Mills and Boon'?

When I popped round that evening there was an eery hush of expectancy over the whole cottage. Her brother told me she was out in the shed with the mother-to-be: alone.

'She wants to handle it on her own,' he told me. But when I told him I'd wait till it was all over he whistled through his teeth and shook his head. 'Ah no, Ducker. You see she's been waiting for you. And she expects, insists that you be present at the birth.'

'What?' I gulped, feeling nauseous already. He was trying very hard not to laugh. 'Who does she think I am? The father?'

He chuckled to himself, stepped aside and guided me gently through the old, stone cottage, out of the kitchen and steered me towards the little wooden maternity shed. It was quite dark there so they'd hung an old oil-lamp on the wall.

She shooshed me up immediately and pulled me to the side of the shed where I could watch this stomach-churning spectacle without being in the way. My paternal presence obviously impressed the goat because she bleated angrily and strutted heavily around, nosing at the straw. She seemed very restless. Perhaps I was a week too early. Lucy stepped closer and hugged my arm, yet having eyes only for her pregnant girlfriend. 'She's building her nest, look,' Lucy whispered, giving my arm a powerful squeeze.

This explained why the animal was nosing the straw into heaps in the corner of the stall, using her hoofs to scrape walls of straw into a sort of semi-circle. God knows how long I stood there, trying not to look at my watch and bending forward to catch Lucy's explanatory whispers, but gradually this deep hush descended on the hut, till it almost looked like a scene from the Bible, the goat standing in its stall bathed in the soft, orange glow of the lamp.

'She's ready,' gasped Lucy and crept forward eagerly to assist with the birth, as they say. If this was supposed to be some kind of lesson for me to watch and learn from I disappointed them. I had to look away at the vital moment and fought to keep my beans-on-toast safe in my stomach. There was a loud, strained bellow, and just out of the corner of my eye I caught sight of something mauve slithering, more liquid than solid, on to the straw. I took a deep breath, smelt goat, straw and a hot, heavy warmth, saw green lights spark around the wooden roof. Then I turned round.

Lucy was kneeling on the straw drying this glistening white bundle of limbs in a towel. As she sat back on her heels proudly, the watchful mother shifted round and began to lick the white kid that was shivering there like a nervous actress on her opening night. Lucy just gazed lovingly at them both, cooing, 'Isn't she lovely, Ducker,' every five seconds.

The poor kid looked more stunned than lovely, but after only five minutes of attentive, maternal licking a million years of instinct started urging the poor thing to get up on its legs: quick, get up, here comes a tiger, watch out for the hyena, get up! And the creature obeyed, struggling up on wobbly, white matchsticks, still looking sort of amazed at everything. As mum continued to lick her offspring I looked across at Lucy-midwife and it was my turn to be amazed.

She was sitting in the straw with floods of tears cascading down her face. 'Oh, Ducker,' she moaned. 'Isn't life beautiful?'

Well, it certainly seemed to get off to a messy, noisy start. I didn't know what to say. So she got up and rushed over, burying her head on my shoulder – she was taller than I was. Still sobbing she said it again: 'Isn't life beautiful!'

'Well, er . . . yeah, sometimes,' I muttered and thankfully we left the mother and kid to carry on with their growing up.

First she cried at the end of 'Mills and Boon', now she cries when her pet goat gives birth. Were all girls like this? Ruthie certainly wasn't.

I told her so up in her room afterwards. On her bedside table was a painted clay model of a goat and kid that she had made in pottery. A brilliant likeness; the hooves were just right. An artist as well.

'You do love me, don't you?' she asked, sitting on the dipping bed beside me. I jerked at the thought of twenty tricky questions again.

'Course I do, Lucy love,' I admitted unconvincingly and gave her a timid hug.

'You never say,' she rebuked and stroked my knee, ran her fingertip over my mouth as if trying to shape the words.

'No? Well, I, er, say it in sign language,' I joked and gave her another significant hug. She suddenly sagged.

'Everything's a joke to you, isn't it?' she sighed, vacantly gazing at a dark chink at the top of her curtains.

'Well, you gotta laugh,' I defended myself. 'I mean you either laugh or cry, these days – You cry, I laugh. Everybody's different, right?'

She didn't reply, or notice that I was getting a bit angry at all this. I kept talking to fill in the pause. 'You know, you truly are amazing,' I said, picking up the model. 'Sometimes I think you're too deep and complicated for a simple soul like me . . .'

I waited to see how she would get out of that one. 'That's because there's an emptiness about you. There's something missing in your life.'

I remembered then Stoney's remark about horoscopes. But there wasn't anything empty about my life. I lived life to the full, even if I did go to bed at ten o'clock.

'Never mind, Ducker,' she soothed, putting a reassuring hand on my shoulder. 'Aunty Lucy will think of something . . .'

After that I thought things were all over between us, but instead they went surprisingly well. We went to Murph's sister's eighteenth birthday, leaving at half-past eleven before anything happened; more summer discos, more prizes, more admirers, with Merv' Pritchard's shadow looming large in the background but coming no closer.

Then one day she turned up at our pub quite unexpectedly. It was a Saturday morning and she was holding a large box with a cloth over it. A present for her boyfriend.

She placed it gently but triumphantly on the kitchen table, much to the fascination of my mother. She liked Lucy, being mad on animals as well and like Lucy's dad dead keen on CND and Green Peace. I heard a soft scuttling sound under the cloth. What was it: not a tarantula!

No, not a tarantula, but as she swept the cloth away like a magician, a little brown-and-white face and black eyes blinked back at me through the bars. A hamster, a Russian hamster.

'There you are,' she announced gently. 'A little pet: that's what you've been waiting for all this time.'

'But I've got a pet,' I protested, putting my arm slyly round her waist. 'You!'

I was hoping Mum would take this hint and beat it, but she was also drooling over this bewildered bundle of fur that clutched the bars with his little, pink hands: longing to be let out, I suppose.

'What are you going to call him?' Mum asked eagerly.

'Comrade Fred!' I christened him instantly. She jerked back in disappointment. Well, would you call your hamster Tchaikovsky, or Mikhail Gorbachev, even if he was a Russian?

Actually Comrade Fred was a good laugh for a pet, and a Russian. She'd bought him in Thornbury on the spur of the moment, she said. We took him up to my room. On the ceiling I'd stuck a Chad saying 'WOT? NO MICHAEL JACKSON?' If I let him out my mother was the only one who could catch him though, thirty minutes later. He was a sucker, was Fred: always headed for the same place – the back of my wardrobe.

But was he the only sucker? How could a furry little four-legged friend be the one thing I was missing in life? Why bring me a present anyway, now and after all this time?

'Pets are an essential part of growing up,' she told me just before she left. 'They teach you things about life, and death, all in a few years too. And other things, like babies and reproduction.'

'Blimey, don't tell me he's a she!' I blurted out in panic. Lucy reassured me that Fred was very macho, and added that she couldn't see me that night because the whole family were going to visit some friends. I believed her.

Sunday morning I was out in the garden sorting some chairs and umbrellas when Davy Cole popped round to tell me about this rave-up barbecue he'd been to with the Young Farmers.

'Ace time, and our dad let me stay till one,' he told me proudly, as I opened and shut this umbrella. He watched in silence for a while. Then he asked, carefully: 'By the way . . . are you still going with er, Lucy Gillimore then?'

As far as I knew. What did he know? I grunted, 'Why?' He shrugged, not wishing to get involved, but I repeated 'Why?' in my toughest voice. He didn't like me getting at him so answered quickly:

'Why? 'Cos she was there with flippin' Pritchard, that's why!'

'How d'you mean, "with"? She told me the whole family was going out,' which wasn't quite true, but I was trying hard not to sound worried.

'The family was there,' he confessed. 'But he wasn't chatting up her mum and dad, was he?'

'How far did he get?' I asked, and now I was worried.

'Dunno,' he muttered. 'They were still there when I left. You know, dancing and smiling.'

'What sort of smile?' I asked, being a glutton for punishment. 'A polite smile, or a "come and get me" smile?'

'Blimey, Ducker, I didn't watch their every move – I was too busy trying to get away from Dolly Skinner!' he shouted back blushing. 'Anyway, Lucy ain't the "come and get me" type, is she?'

For a moment this red-hot poker that had been hissing inside my guts withdrew itself. I wondered now if Fred was a farewell present. Over the hedge I saw Dolly Skinner's thin grinning face as she cycled towards her true love. They pedalled off together, to the Deer Park, leaving me in the empty garden alone with my doubts and fears.

However, before I'd stopped chuckling at Davy's doom with Dolly Skinner, Gary Streeter came strolling along. He was really depressed at the thought of starting school in a week's time. So he got his own back by depressing me.

'By the way, Ducker – bad luck about Lucy, eh?' He'd stayed there till three o'clock, so could tell me that Lucy's parents had gone by then, leaving her there with her brother, dancing till dawn – with Merv' of course.

'I bet he hasn't got a hamster,' I growled enigmatically. 'Just a rat, or a polecat!'

Gary, seeing how his bad news had struck home, wandered off feeling very pleased with himself, leaving me alone with a long bayonet planted in my guts: it had saw-teeth and was twisting slowly.

I had to talk about it, to discuss this problem with somebody. Dad was useless, he'd just quote old Biblical phrases like 'all's fair in love and war,' or 'faint heart never won fair lady'. Oh sure. Either that or write to Claire Rayner – calling myself Gary Streeter, of course. But she'd just say, 'forget the heartbreak, love, you're young enough to start again and find somebody new.' Oh yeah.

I neither saw Lucy, nor phoned her for two days. Worse, far worse than that – she didn't phone me. I cycled past her cottage on the green one evening. No goat, no girl. She was probably in the pub playing pinball with Merv'.

I ended up discussing my problem in the school tennis courts one morning. I was umpire, while Gary and Murph were serving doubles and doing McEnroe impressions. Murph was actually quite sympathetic, having had the same problem three weeks ago, except that she was seventeen! They both had hairier legs than me too. Come to think of it Murph had hairier legs than King Kong.

'Do you know what she said to me?' I asked as Murph prepared to serve. They both guessed, wrongly. 'She said to me she felt like a woman.' Murph tapped the ball thoughtfully. 'Then she said she wanted to be loved like a woman. Imagine that . . .'

Murph stood up straight, swung up his racket and puffed out his cheeks, very impressed. 'She said what? You lucky little sod!'

'Yeah, but what did you say, Ducker?' asked Gary knowingly.

'I fed the goat,' I announced, looking down at my worn trainers.

Murph's eyes widened. 'Fed the goat? That's a good way of putting it!'

'How else should I put it?' I wailed full of self pity. 'I gave it grass.'

'Gave it grass,' Murphy repeated and chuckled lustily. He bent over the serving line, then straightened up again. 'You mean you really *did* feed the goat? And that's all?'

'I just said I did, didn't I?'

'No wonder she went off with Merv' then,' Gary jeered, giving the bayonet a sharp twist. There was a long pause as they carried on with their game. Murph served just out but I called it 'in'. I was only half-watching; my mind clouding with black, murderous thoughts. The ball socked the net twice and Murph's racket flew into the fence.

'Nothing left for it,' said Gary as he waited for his partner to regain his 'cool'. 'If you feel really bad about it, it's a question of honour. You'll have to fight him for her.'

Big joke. They both laughed.

'Yeah, Ducker,' Gary continued. 'If you stood on a chair, you might just reach him.'

. But I wasn't really the violent type. Not yet anyway. I'd never been to a football match. I stopped plotting blood-curdling revenge and stewed in my own poison till the set finished. Murph lost, six-love!

No, I would do the next best thing. She would cease to exist. From now on I would ignore that long-legged goat-girl Gemini with two-faces, and save my attention for the second and third years who sat on the dossers' bench under the Town Hall clock.

That evening as I sprayed lighter fuel deodorant under my arms and winced in agony, preparing to cycle off to the girls outside the town hall, who should come knocking on my door but She-who-no-longer-existed. Whats hername.

She strode in, straight past me and began to tap the bars of the Lubianka, trying to wake Comrade Fred, talking to the motionless, nocturnal bundle in his paper nest in the corner. My flipping mother had let her in, for some reason.

'How's it going then, Fred?' she asked. 'Your master keeps ignoring me for some reason, so I thought I'd come and see how you were for myself.'

Neither of us moved, nor answered. You-know-who continued.

'Somebody told me he was jealous, Fred, jealous be-cause I spent the night with another boy!'

Any more of this and if Fred didn't bite her I would.

'If there's one thing I can't stand, it's jealousy; can you, Fred. Especially if it's not deserved.'

A pity I wasn't a ventriloquist. He could have given her a really rude answer. 'Of course, I didn't tell him the truth about Saturday in case he got jealous. Didn't work though, did it?'

Fred began to rustle uncertainly. She may have been telling the truth, I suppose.

'I mean, you'd think after going out with someone for two months he'd know you well enough to trust you, eh Fred? But oh no, not your little master: he thinks I was having it off in the bushes all night.'

'So what were you doing till four o'clock then, playing Happy Families?' I snarled. She swung round and glared back at me.

'We talked, and talked, and danced, and then – we talked. O.K.?'

'Talked?' I laughed in disbelief. 'I bet Merv' enjoyed that. He's a great conversationalist.'

'Well, no, not quite,' she remembered more clearly. 'First he moaned about stubble-burning for ten minutes, then he went off and got drunk with his mates.'

'What did he get drunk for?' I asked suspiciously.

Her shoulders raised in a heavy sigh of disbelief. 'Because they wouldn't play his favourite record, that's why.'

'But why didn't you take me along then?' I asked still angry.

'For one thing Merv' invited me and told me to leave you at home,' she began. 'For another I know your parents wouldn't let you stay later than half-eleven, so I didn't want to cause trouble for you, or hurt his feelings . . . you know . . .'

She shrugged as if that was all there was to it. As if being honest was enough. Hurt his feelings? Why was she more worried about his feelings than my feelings?

'You didn't have to go with him,' I persisted. She pulled a face.

'I didn't want to say no . . . you know . . .' All I knew was that it was not the safest attitude to have. But I began to relent.

'Go for a stroll?' I asked as a peace offering. She agreed. We wandered across the road, arm in arm, but not speaking. It was a mellow golden evening, ringing with birdsong. I used to think they sang for the love of it, till we learnt in Science that they were shouting insults at their rivals. Nice insults though.

We passed the school: emptiness reflected from the windows. Then we strolled down this farm track that ran parallel to the school field and led into a leafy, country lane.

'You're not still in a bad mood, are you?' she asked finally. I grunted and sought an excuse.

'Living in the country's so boring,' I complained. 'I mean listen to that flipping bird up there for a start.' Deep in the green wood beside the lane this bird was chipping away at the same repetitive note, like a tin hammer on a block of granite.

'That's only a chiffchaff,' the country-girl identified for the ex-townie.

'They are a bit boring, but . . . listen . . .' She hugged my arm imploringly – I had my hands in my pockets. On the other side of the lane another, larger bird had started singing this powerfully-warbled melody. Very nice; if you're in the mood. 'There, Ducker, a blackbird – doesn't she sing lovely?'

'Beautiful! If we had twenty-three more we could bake a pie,' I muttered.

The bird took my witty hint, shut itself up and flew deeper into the wood, though we couldn't see it.

'Don't be horrible. See, you scared him away,' she wailed. But undeterred by threats of baking, the bird started his loud trilling song again. Lucy stood stock-still. 'Hold on, Ducker . . . no, listen: that's not a blackbird!' She glanced at her watch for some reason. 'Ducker,' she whispered almost in a religious awe. 'Ducker, it's a nightingale . . .'

'At this time of day?' I scoffed. 'Where is he then?'

'You won't see him: they hide away in the deepest part of tree or bush. And they do sing in the evening sometimes. Listen, Ducker; this could be a once in a lifetime experience . . .'

'Once in a lifetime,' I repeated unexcitedly. 'Yeah, and you know, if I was a poet, I'd be really inspired by all this beauty . . .'

She gave me a funny, sidelong look and waited for my piece of inspiration.

'The countryside's a pleasant place,
The woods are green and leafy,
I still wish I was back in town,
Where the women weren't so beefy . . .'

She didn't laugh, or clap. This wasn't the same as our first stroll. For one thing I felt she was just doing it to be nice to me – out of sympathy or guilt perhaps.

'You mean, all you did till four-thirty was chat and dance?' I asked suddenly. She stood for a moment grinding her teeth.

'No; after my parents went, all the lads put their car-keys in a pile on the grass. Then each girl picked a bunch of car-keys and went off with the bloke. Then half an hour later, someone blew a whistle and we started all over again. OK?'

She had to be joking. This was worse than my worst nightmare. No, whatever did happen that night, this wasn't love any more; this was a gentle leg-pulling out of sympathy.

We turned and walked back up the lane, past the school field where swallows were flying low over the damp grass; their white bellies skimming and hissing over the newly laid-out rugby pitch. I hated rugby: the cold white H made me think of winter, mud and freezing in the rain.

She pecked my cheek and told me to give my love to Fred.

'Lucy sends you her love, Fred,' I told him as he stood blinking at me eagerly and clutching the cold steel bars of his cage. He looked up at the door in the roof. I still couldn't work out why this furry, striped acrobat, struggling to get out of his prison, was supposed to fill some gap in my life. Probably guilty conscience, I thought, as he crouched at the edge of his cage and sniffed the air, testing it with his whiskers before the big jump. Splat! Down he went on the lino. Whiz! Under the bed. He'd better watch out for my feet too.

Before I knew it, term would be starting. A new syllabus with real exams at the end of it. The Big One. I dreaded all the long afternoons of greying clouds, heavy eyelids, roller boards squeaking in endless torment, round and round. So, I lay back on the bed and stared up at bits of Sellotape on the ceiling, making my den look tattier than ever. As I heard Fred scrambling up the North Face of the Eiger, I wondered if he should carry a hammer and sickle in his snout. He was certainly non- stop entertainment, but that couldn't be what she meant. Anyway, I wasn't in love any more so I didn't care.

She must have outgrown me. We'd both outgrown 'Mills and Boon'. And by the time I'd caught up with her in four years' time I'd have outgrown love itself.

I couldn't wait.

Fred peered down at me triumphantly from the top of the wardrobe. 'Mum!' I shouted down the stairs into the kitchen. 'Fred's up there again!'

At least one of us was a success in life.

MICHAEL A. PEARSON

Ultima Thule

There is no joy like the joy of being twenty-two, success-fully beginning a career as a commercial artist and being committed – Elizabeth found the word 'engaged' too old-fashioned – to the man she had set her sights on for the past three years. So she thought, at the time he made the suggestion that they should take a brief holiday to the country property of his old friend, Emlyn Jones.

'I want him to meet you,' Richard had said. 'I am proud of you, and I want to show you off. And to me he is the person who matters most. Besides, he hasn't long to live.'

Even if she had wanted to, she could not have refused. Richard, as usual, had given two reasons she found un-answerable. But she had no intention of refusing. It seemed to her the ultimate delight in a series of mounting joys. She did not know then that there are joys, but of a different kind, equally profound but more intoxicating because, like a flower or a cloud, ephemeral.

Her holidays were due and he, as junior but very pro-mising partner of an architectural firm, could more or less arrange his work to suit himself. So he picked her up from work one Friday afternoon and they made their way out of the city just a little ahead of the peak-hour traffic. He had told her she had a flair for clothes, so she had dressed with care. She now sat contentedly beside him, watching his profile as he manoeuvred the Porsche through busy streets and out to meet the motorway. He talked as he drove, his face, with its bones so prominent, animated and alert. She looked at the long, strong hands on the wheel and knew that she was committed irrevocably to everything about him. Her tastes were always towards older, intelligent and sophisticated men. The eight years between them was, she thought, just right.

Her long, contented sigh made him turn and look at her. 'Tired?'

'Just happy.'

He smiled, and it was not until they were in the open country that he spoke again. 'You haven't asked me a single question about Emlyn.'

'Who's Emlyn?'

'Elizabeth!' It was a mild reproach, but she felt immediately guilty.

'It was enough that we were going on a holiday together.'

'Nevertheless.' The winter night was beginning to close in and he switched on the lights. They drove down a golden tunnel, the two of them, enclosed in their small capsule, intimate and alone. 'Emlyn is your host. He is an old man, and he was my professor when I was studying. He is lonely because his wife has died and his family have flown to different countries for different reasons. Also, I told you he hasn't long to live. He has developed diabetes in his old age, together with a few other things. So he has chosen to retire to this rather isolated property where, I understand, faithful retainers manage to earn him enough to keep the place a going concern. He suggested I should bring you up because, knowing you are by way of being artistic –'

'Thank you.' Elizabeth's voice was less than enthusiastic.

' – he thought you would enjoy some of the more dramatic views of the mountains that are available from Ultima
Thule.'

'Ultima Thule?'

'I don't have to teach you latin, surely? The name of his
property.' She was silent, and he went on, 'Also, I think he is
lonely, and he said he wanted to see the woman of my
choice. You will like him. I think I can say I love him.'

The car sped on, smooth and silent, and the night flowed
away behind them. Every so often the lights of a town flared
up, twinkled, flashed and died away. Once a train roared
under them as the road leapt the permanent way. They went
deeper into remote and secret hills.

It was late when the car stopped at a wide iron gate that
said, Ultima Thule. Elizabeth had been almost asleep, but
now the silence hummed in her ears. Richard said gently,
'Do you feel up to opening it?'

She fumbled at the catch, swung the door wide and stepped
out stiffly. The air, cold, sharp, aromatic, caught her un-
awares. At once she was fully awake, conscious of a vast
expanse above her head across which stars were flung like
seeds from some primitive celestial sower. The only ground
she could see was directly in front, illuminated by the
headlights. She found the catch and swung the gate open.

'Mind where you put your feet.'

'What?'

'We're in the country now,' he said, and laughed.
'Cowpats.'

She saw them then, mounds like small dark boulders, and
more ominous splashes on the track. She wiped her shoes in
the grass and got in. 'I don't mind,' she said defiantly. 'I even
like the smell.'

He kissed her quickly. 'You are my Elizabeth,' he said,
and drove on.

They saw the hous ⸻ e time before they reached it – a glow of light on a dar ⸻ almost invisible hillside. After two ramps and one lengthy delay while some sheep, camped on the warm earth of the track, moved themselves off, they passed through a gateway. At once they were conscious of trees pressing in around them. They turned a corner and were at the front door. It was wide open and light flooded out on to worn steps. Silhouetted in the doorway stood their host. 'Thought you'd come the front way,' he said. 'Us country folk always use the back.' Looking at him carefully, she knew immediately why Richard liked him so much. A kind, gentle man, with a pleasant voice and shrewd eyes. As she climbed out into the scent of the big conifers she knew she had done right to come.

Next morning when they woke to a misty and silent world that later turned to a wet and dripping world, she was content to sit watching the small flames and the rosy glow of big logs in the fireplace while Richard and Emlyn talked. Once, hearing what seemed to her a quite terrifying uproar outside, she went to the window. A herd of black cattle was moving along the track past the garden fence. Every beast appeared to be bellowing and above the bellowing were the shouts of men. As she watched, one beast broke away and headed with determination for the open country. It was followed at once by a man on a horse. After a short, sharp burst of speed he managed to block it, turning his horse on its hind legs and cracking a long whip in its face. It swung back and the horseman followed it until it rejoined the herd.

'Good man, Jack,' said Emlyn's voice behind her. 'There aren't many left who can use a stockwhip like that these days.'

She continued to watch as the herd, still bellowing,

moved down the track past the homestead and out on to
the plain. Three horsemen rode behind them. One of
them, sitting so easily in the saddle, was the good man,
Jack. She saw now that he was quite young, and she
watched him until he was out of sight.

When the following morning revealed a clear sky and a
spectacular mountainous landscape drowned in sunshine,
their idleness was at an end. 'I've arranged for you to go
out for the day,' Emlyn said at breakfast. 'There's a place I
particularly want Elizabeth to see. It's something I've had
in mind since we arranged that you should come, and
because it involves a view like no other view you've ever
seen, it has to be a fine day. My man, Jack – the one you
saw yesterday with the cattle – will be round with the
four-wheel drive in about –' he looked at his watch, 'half
an hour. There's lunch ready to take, and you must be
prepared for quite a walk. The vehicle track peters out
after a while. It's rough going, but Jack will be with you to
keep an eye on you.'

'Yes, but –' Richard began, and stopped.

'There'll be time for solitary walks later.'

'I didn't mean that. I was going to say –' Richard looked
at him in mild reproof, 'can't we have you with us?'

'Too much for me now, I'm afraid.' He hesitated, and
then said briskly, 'But it's something you mustn't miss.
And today's the day. The weather's perfect.'

The four-wheel drive turned out to be an ancient Landrover, apparently held together with string and wire.
Seeing Richard's eye running over its vital parts, Emlyn
said, 'Don't judge it by its looks. It'll get you there and
back all right, won't it, Jack?'

Jack was as tall and thin as he had seemed yesterday
when glued to his horse, and he had obviously spent his
life out in the weather. He seemed, in fact, to have been

through very similar experiences to the Landrover. 'That's right,' he said, and smiled at his boss. The smile revealed a surprising warmth of affection.

It was a long, rough drive. At first they crossed open paddocks and a few creeks. Then the scrub became thicker and the ground less even. They found themselves winding round the sides of hills, climbing with agonized sounds from the Landrover up the slopes of gullies. Every so often the scrub and the trees would fall back and they would get a glimpse of an expanse of rolling country opening out below them.

The track had become noticeably worse and the trees were thickening when they came, suddenly, to a rock wall that allowed no passage. Jack stopped the Landrover and for the first time spoke. 'It's a long walk. Boss told you, did he?'

Richard had got out and now stood looking about him. 'He warned us. We're tougher than we might look, aren't we, Elizabeth?'

Inexplicably she was embarrassed. 'I hope so,' she said, and looked at Jack.

He was regarding her gravely, apparently summing up her capacity for punishment. Then he nodded. 'OK. This way.' He walked off to where the track began at one end of the rock wall. They fell in behind him, Elizabeth and then Richard. As they climbed she watched his slow, effortless steps upward. Behind her, Richard followed easily enough, but here in this wild, beautiful, unfriendly countryside, Jack was at home. Richard was the outsider.

They walked for some time in silence, Jack because he had nothing he thought it was necessary to say, Richard and Elizabeth because they had little breath to spare for talking. All round them the life of the scrub-covered hills, of bird and insect, went on – busy, noisy, preoccupied.

They emerged on to a length of track where the hillside fell away suddenly on their left, devoid of trees and undergrowth, where a recent landslide had carried them down with it. Far below lay the countryside they had left. Cattle looked like a scattering of black lozenges and sheep like tufts of fluff. Jack stopped and pointed.

'What a view,' Elizabeth said, breathless.

'No. I mean – look there.' He pointed to the empty air halfway between earth and sky.

'It's a bird,' said Richard.

'It's a wedgetail,' said Jack.

Elizabeth saw it then – dark against the blue sky, huge wings outstretched, motionless. 'It's an eagle,' she said.

'Wedgetail,' said Jack again. 'Poisoned rabbits nearly did for them. But they're coming back. I like to see them.' It was the longest speech he had made so far. He turned and continued on.

They came at last to a place where the track turned into a series of rough steps formed by the uneven stones. Jack stopped. He looked first at Richard's feet and then at Elizabeth's. 'Should've checked before.' He sounded vaguely apologetic. 'Boots OK, are they? We got to climb a bit here.' Suddenly he smiled. 'We're near the top, but.'

It was a short, stiff climb and twice in the course of it Richard had to pull Elizabeth up where her legs were not long enough easily to span the stretch. Jack went slowly on and did not look back. It was near the top, when the worst seemed over and attention had slackened that the accident happened. Elizabeth, looking up, and not down where her feet were, put her boot on a firm-looking but treacherous rock and it rolled with her, sending her suddenly headlong past Richard, halfway down the slope. When she tried to pick herself up a stab of acute pain in her ankle made her yelp and stay where she was. She lay, head down, not daring to move. Richard reached her in two enormous strides, his arms held out to pick her up. He was checked by a shout from Jack.

'Leave her be.' There was a scattering of pebbles and Jack slid down behind him. 'If something's broke –' he said, and bent down. She looked up and did her best to smile. 'Hurts, does it? Where?'

She looked up at Richard. 'I'm so sorry, Richard.'

'My poor girl, you could hardly –'

She forgot what Richard was saying as steady fingers pressed her ankle. She gasped as they found the damage. The fingers stopped their investigation at once, but after a moment began again very gently to probe the ankle joint. 'Tell me where it hurts.' She told him, and soon he stood up. He turned to Richard. 'Don't think it's broke. Just sprained, probably. She'll have to be got back to the vehicle. But I better bandage it before it swells.' He stopped, hesitated, and said, 'Or do you think you'd better –?'

'Oh no,' said Richard quickly. 'I think if you're experienced in this sort of thing it would be better if you did it.' For the first time, Elizabeth saw him at a loss. Here, it seemed, were his limits.

'OK.' Jack looked at Elizabeth, looked again at Richard and then said, 'Look, it's only a few minutes to the top. You can't miss the track now. Have a look, take your pictures, and I'll get the leg bound up.'

'Oh, I don't think –'

'Richard, please go. I won't feel so badly if I think you've got there. I feel such a –' She gasped again as she felt her leg lifted, 'a heel, letting you down. Please, Richard.' It was an effort to keep her voice steady.

'If you're sure? I'll be quick, then.'

It was not until he was out of sight that she thought to

say, 'What will you use to bandage it? Had you better call him back?'

He had been rolling back the leg of her jeans, but now he looked up and she saw again the quick creasing of the small lines round his eyes as he smiled. 'Reckon I'll find something.'

Quite soon it was done. Miraculously from somewhere he had produced a bandage, which he now damped with water from the water bottle he was carrying. 'Always carry one,' he said when she asked. 'When I take the boss's visitors out. You never know.'

A good deal of the pain had gone from her ankle, and she no longer had to brace herself to bear it. She tried to move, but at once felt his hands on her shoulders, holding her down. 'Steady on. We'll wait till you – till Richard comes back an' then we'll lift you together.'

'But I'll have to get back to the Landrover. I'll have to –'

He shook his head. 'You put that foot on the ground and you'll know it pretty quick. It won't do it any good, either.'

'But how can I – how can you – oh, dear, now I'm being such a nuisance.' The tears that suddenly poured down her cheeks filled her with dreadful shame.

'Here. There's no need to cry about it.' She found her shoulder patted and stroked as if she were a distressed puppy. It was curiously comforting. 'It's the shock, see? Often takes you like that.'

She was still gulping when they heard Richard's footsteps on the track above. She clutched his wrist. 'Don't let him see me like this.' And she dragged her sleeve quickly across her wet cheeks. But there had been gravel rash on the palm of her hand and it had bled on to her sleeve and it was now, alarmingly, all over her face

Also, the carefully applied mascara had run. The overall effect brought a short, quickly stifled sound from Jack. 'What's the matter? What are you looking at?'

He swallowed and said, 'Nothing. Here. Just a minute.' He fished in his pocket, produced a clean coloured handkerchief, leaned forward and gently wiped her face. The smile lingered in the creases round his eyes.

'Why am I so funny?' She was deeply hurt.

He shook his head and, overcome by the recollection, burst out laughing. 'Sorry,' he said at last. 'Reckon it was all that blood an' all that black stuff.'

Reluctantly she found herself smiling at him. 'Is it all right now?'

He nodded and pressed the handkerchief into her hand. 'It's OK. Here, better keep this.' He stood up as Richard clattered down to them.

'I got some wonderful shots. It's magnificent. Elizabeth, I wish you could – how's the leg? My poor girl.' He bent down, put his hand on her knee, jolting the ankle very slightly. 'You're a bit pale. Are you all right?' She nodded, not quite trusting herself to speak. 'And now, how do we get her back? Carry her between us?' He turned to Jack. 'I suppose she shouldn't try to walk.'

'She can't walk.' There was a sudden authority in Jack's voice. 'First, we'll get her up.'

They lifted her between them. 'Don't put that foot down,' Jack said when she was upright. 'Put your hand on my shoulder and stand on the other one.' His shoulder was as firm as a rock.

They tried lifting her between them, but immediately the difference in their height became an obstacle, and Richard's feet on the rough ground were not as firm as Jack's. Once or twice as they proceeded, crablike, down the track she had to stifle a gasp of pain. At last Jack stopped. 'Hold on. This isn't too good.' They stopped and carefully let her down. She clung to Jack's shoulder.

Richard was breathing hard. He looked worried. 'Elizabeth, is it very painful? Think you can hold out? I suppose there'd have to be some other way we could get down?' And he looked at Jack.

She knew that this way she could not hold out, and it was clear to her that Richard could not, either. For the first time she felt sorry for him. She also knew that Richard would not be able to say, 'This is too much for me,' and was about to say it for him, regardless of his pride, when Jack said, 'It'll hurt less if I carry her on my back.' He might have said it as much for Richard's sake as for her own.

'Can you?' said Richard. Undeniably there was relief in his tone.

Between the three of them and without too much pain to her ankle they got her on to his back, his arms under her knees, hers round his neck. 'That's better,' he said, and straightened his legs as if she were no weight at all.

At first she could think of nothing but the trouble she was causing, the disappointment Richard must be feeling that she had let him down. Guilt, and a certain shame kept her silent. Then a new thought presented itself and she said, 'Aren't I too heavy?'

The vibrations of Jack's laugh reached her through the back of his shirt. 'Reckon you weigh less than a sack of wheat and I've carried plenty of them.' She seemed to cause him constant amusement.

By the time they reached the Landrover a worse damage than the sprained ankle had been done. Elizabeth would not have put it like that. A curious, deep contentment had come over her, something like the feeling she had experienced as she had tramped upward, her feet in his

footsteps, behind him. All she had needed to complete
the picture had been a bundle on her back containing pots
and kettles. But she was still far from putting her present
state into words. All she knew – and knew with certainty
– was that all her values had suddenly changed. There
was only one thing that mattered now. She was in every
sense transported.

It was a long, painful journey home. Whenever
Richard asked if the ankle hurt she lied and said it did
not. But she looked at Jack for the brief nod and smile
that told her all was well and that there would soon be an
end to the pain.

When they reached the homestead Emlyn looked at
Jack, too. 'What do you think, Jack? X-ray?'

'I reckon. So we know for sure. I could take her in
now if you like. Get it over.'

'I think that's my job,' Richard said quickly. 'I'll bring
the car round.'

But in the end it was Emlyn's big, comfortable car that
accommodated her best. When the front seat was lowered
so that the leg could be raised there was little room for
anyone else in the car. Her last sight of Richard was of his
face peering at her through the window. It wore an
expression she had not seen before, but for once she failed
to notice.

Because there was no better way of getting her from
the car to the casualty ward, he carried her again.
'Richard couldn't have carried me in,' she said as he lifted
her out of the car.

'Reckon he could if he had to. It's easy for me. I been
doing it all my life.'

She had her arm round his neck. Now she clung more
tightly. 'Don't leave me, Jack.'

He looked surprised, and then he laughed. 'I'm not

leaving you. I'll be waiting to take you back. What do you think?'

She had not intended to say it, and it was not what she had meant, anyway. But she thought – she hoped – his arm had tightened a little round her as she said it. She looked up into his face, but he was concentrating on getting her feet through the door without hurting them.

The doctor who attended to her hurt her more than Jack had done. But the X-ray showed no break, and after a rebandaging they took her back to him. She had hoped he would carry her to the car, but he was standing there waiting, holding a pair of crutches.

'I got these,' he said, and gravely handed them to her. 'See if you can use them. Try them now.'

'But I can't –' She looked up at him, and her expression was more revealing than she knew. 'Please, Jack.' She tried, unsuccessfully, to smile.

There was no answering smile. Instead he thrust the crutches into her hands and said more roughly than she had heard him speak, 'Try them. You can get out to the car with them.'

She reached for them, then in silence and awkwardly took step after difficult step out from the hospital while he held the door for her, across the footpath until she stood by the door of the car. It seemed to her a cruel thing, but she did not know he had been one step behind, ready to catch her if the crutch slipped. He lifted her into the car, and only spoke once before sliding into the driver's seat. 'Are you comfortable?' She nodded because for the moment she could not speak.

They stopped at the boundary gate and he got out to open it. But when he had driven through and shut it again he did not immediately drive on. Instead he turned towards her and took her two hands in his, and the white, lacquer-tipped fingers lay in his hard, brown palm. He seemed to be studying her hands as he spoke, rubbing the backs of them with his thumb. He said, 'You didn't ought to make it this hard for me to do my job.' Her hands seemed to mesmerize him, for he sat staring at them for some time until, still without looking at her, he put them back on her lap, started the car and drove on. She did not hear him speak again until the end of her visit.

When they reached the homestead he gave Emlyn the doctor's report and took the car away at once. She was left facing the steps balanced precariously on the crutches. She had started to climb them by the time Richard reached her. 'He should have helped you up the steps,' he said and she knew he was furious.

'I am to learn to use the crutches,' she said, suddenly defiant. 'Leave me alone, Richard.'

The next few days were spent getting used to the crutches. Jack came every day, but she never saw him. 'He comes for his instructions,' Emlyn told her. 'And he always asks after you.' He thought it unnecessary to say this had not been Jack's usual practice. There was a tension in the air now that he was well aware of, and of its cause. Because he had a great affection for Richard and because he was disposed to like Elizabeth, and also because he felt more than a little responsible, he kept his counsel and made what moves he could to defuse a situation he recognized as explosive.

So Elizabeth saw no more of Jack, but Emlyn drove them out on fine days, talked a lot and offered what distractions he could. And he saw that Richard began to lose that first pinched look about the mouth. They all, silently and for different reasons, began to count the days until the end of the visit.

It came at last, and Elizabeth heard Emlyn say, as they

sat by the fire one night, 'What time are you and Elizabeth planning to leave tomorrow, Richard?'

It was a long night, and she did not sleep. Feverishly scheming, she was wide awake when the sun rose on the first spring day. She got up early and silently left the house. Because she was still on crutches she could not go far, but she was able to reach a small bench near the machinery shed, and was sitting there when Jack came round the corner to start work. When he saw her he stopped dead. She held out his handkerchief, washed and ironed. 'I wanted to give you back your handkerchief. I'm sorry I had it so long.'

He came up to her slowly and took it from her. But at the same time he was fishing in his shirt pocket. He pulled out some battered photographs and handed them to her. 'Thought I might see you some time. Wanted to show you these. My kids.' He looked worried and he was frowning as he handed them to her.

Automatically she took them, and automatically began to look at them. Slowly it came to her that these – these tattered, dirty, cheerful children were his children. She peered more closely. They were like him. One – a boy – was very like him, even to the curious little smile round his eyes. She held it up. 'Can I have this one?'

He looked surprised, and hesitated. Then he said, 'Sure. Sure; you keep it if you want. That's Bobby. He's a trick of a kid. Seven, he is.'

She gave the others back and he returned them to his pocket. For a moment he stood quite still. Then he said, ''Bye, Elizabeth,' and walked past her. It seemed he had not seen the hand she held out to him, but as he passed she felt the palm of his hand rest briefly on the top of her head.

Later that morning Richard drove her home. He knew she was scarcely aware of his presence. She did not speak at all, and all the long drive back he made no attempt to break the silence. He was thinking, in fact, of Emlyn's last words to him. 'Don't worry too much. Give her time. It will be all right.'

Six months later he was with Elizabeth again. He was handing her a ring. 'I know it's old-fashioned and all that, but I'd like you to have it. Even if –'

She saw that, for once, he could not go on. She took the ring and put it on. Then she kissed him. 'You see,' she said, 'I put it on *myself*. That's the difference. Oh, Richard, you've been so good, so kind, so patient.'

Suddenly he stood up. 'I need a drink. Elizabeth, you don't know –'

'Yes, I do,' she wanted to say. But the past six months, if they had not given her what she thought was her heart's desire, had taught her things about herself – and others – that were more valuable, and she said instead, 'There's nothing I need to know. All's well, Richard.' And she came towards him.

JOAN PHIPSON

The Authors

Vivien Alcock's most recent novels are *The Mysterious Mr Ross* (1987) and *The Cuckoo Sister* (1985), which was successfully dramatised for television in 1986. She feels that 'It is difficult to write a story without love coming into it somewhere. Like the common cold, there's so much of it about.'

Anthony Masters' most recent teenage novel is *Badger* (1986). He writes: 'I have always thought that a love story should contain moments of ecstasy and moments of pain. At least – that is how love has always happened to me. Perhaps it is the way it should always happen. Then we know when we are in love.'

Mollie Hunter writes: 'I started writing at nine years old, fell in love at sixteen, and married the bloke at eighteen; since when we've had two sons and three grandsons. My personal productions have been twenty-five books, one of which, *A Sound of Chariots*, includes the true story of the great, romantic love between my parents. In our more than forty years of happy marriage, also, I've often been deeply moved to witness the new generation's discovery of the pains and pleasures of love, and this feeling has further inspired much that has gone into others of my books. I'm a strong supporter, indeed, of romance in fiction, but only providing that, instead of being portrayed in some soft-focus fantasy, it's shown in the way that romance so often and so gloriously does happen in the real lives of real people.'

Berlie Doherty's most recent novel for teenagers is *Granny Was a Buffer Girl* (1986). She writes: 'I was born in Knotty Ash, in Liverpool, and it was there that I had my first romance. I let the boy over the road kiss me because he let me have a go on his trike. But I was only four at the time, and such transactions seemed quite natural to me, and I suppose it took me a few years to learn that there was a bit more to love than that. I spent most of my childhood on the Wirral coast, 'over the water' from Liverpool. This is where 'Summer of Ladybirds' is set, even though I now live in Sheffield. Red Rocks was a very special place to me when I was a teenager, but I have to confess that I lied about the camp site. There are many ways to write about love, because love shows itself in many ways, and in this story I decided to move away from romance and look at tenderness. That can be a very powerful emotion, and is very close to love. Most of us fall in love at some time or another, but it doesn't always have a happy ending. But perhaps you'd like to think about that for yourselves. What *is* a happy ending?'

Alison Prince's most recent novels for teenagers are *The Others* (1986) and *Nick's October* (1986). She has done a wide variety of jobs, including teaching and running a smallholding in Suffolk, but now that her three children are grown up, she lives on the island of Arran, off the west coast of Scotland. The love story, she feels, is much abused, often reduced to conventional sentimentality. Love is, she says, probably the most overwhelming experience which many people ever undergo, and for each individual it comes as a new and totally unique experience. As such, it remains for the writer an eternal and powerful theme.

Michael A. Pearson writes: 'Michael Anthony Pearson, the son of a Bristol butcher, was born eight years after Cliff Richard. He was educated at Sefton Park Primary and the Bristol Grammar School for boys – an experience from which he is only just recovering! He graduated from Bristol University with a rather good degree but allowed the careers officer to talk him into the teaching profession. He believes that, generally, co-education is a good thing provided the girls don't let themselves get pushed around. He taught for ten years at Berkeley Vale Comprehensive School, where, he says, the girls were more than a match for the boys. About Love itself, he feels more realistic than romantic: it can be 'the best of times or the worst of times', to quote somebody famous. He believes that one day women will rule the world and his hobbies include music, West Country Rugby, photography, bird-watching and marking homework. After ten years of writing radio stories for the BBC he began to publish children's books: *Winners and Losers*, *The Bubble Gum Champion*, and *Splashers* (1987), all set in and around a mythical Gloucestershire Comprehensive school called Swanswell.'

Joan Phipson's most recent teenage novels are *The Watcher in the Garden* (1983) and *Hit and Run* (1986). She writes: 'Although I travelled a good deal when I was a child, I have lived on a farm in the Australian countryside for some thirty years now. The fact that I write mainly for children is due, I believe, to my vividly remembered childhood. But the reason that so many of my stories have a rural setting – and one not dissimilar from the place where I live – is because this is the kind of place I know best. I know it in all its seasons, in all kinds of climate, and its effect on the people that live here. This is an important prerequisite in any story that is to ring true. When one uses the term 'love story' one usually has in mind the slight, formula-based tale of boy meets girl/boy parted from girl/boy reunited with girl. It is as well to remember that physical love is one of the most powerful of human emotions, and that much of the great literature of the world is based on it. For instance: *The Song of Solomon*, *Romeo and Juliet* and *Anna Karenina*, to mention only one in a variety of genre.'